The
Happening

The Happening

A Carol for All Seasons

JOHN WAHTERA

AN ATLANTIC MONTHLY PRESS BOOK
Little, Brown and Company · Boston · Toronto

FIRST EDITION

T 11/74

This book appeared in *Redbook* in slightly different form.

ATLANTIC–LITTLE, BROWN BOOKS

ARE PUBLISHED BY

LITTLE, BROWN AND COMPANY

IN ASSOCIATION WITH

THE ATLANTIC MONTHLY PRESS

LIBRARY OF CONGRESS CATALOGING IN PUBLICATION DATA

Wahtera, John.
  The happening; a carol for all seasons.

  "An Atlantic Monthly Press book."
  I. Title.
PZ4.W1374Hap3 [PS3573.A395]   813'.5'4   74–10830
ISBN 0–316–917508

Designed by Susan Windheim
Published simultaneously in Canada
by Little, Brown & Company (Canada) Limited

PRINTED IN THE UNITED STATES OF AMERICA

For Lilli, a believer.

The
Happening

Chapter 1

The Joyous Season, as it became more hysterical, also became much colder. Monotonous day followed monotonous day, dawning with skies as gray and gritty as city snow, though as yet no snow had fallen. But on a day late in December, a premature twilight fell over the city, irrevocably promising snow. Through the last light of that day a solitary figure, carrying a large canvas, made its way through the glittering avenues of the city's main park. The figure paused momentarily to consider the chipped plaster images of a manger scene and then left the paved walkway, going directly to a line of wire pens thrown up as temporary quarters for a herd of rented deer. The deer had been in residence a month now, and though the city was paying rental on white deer, they had become a yellowish brown in color. The fences, which had been tight enough a month ago, were

3

all bent inward by the daily crush of children brought there to see the deer.

"Ho-ho-ho, Rudolph," the figure said.

Rudolph lifted his head in mild curiosity at the tall stranger in the loose parka. From a safe distance on his side of the fence, he stared impassively at the shaggy-haired visitor leaning over the fence offering him a handful of wilted lettuce. A hundred times a day Rudolph was offered sticks, candy wrappers, oak leaves; a conditioned cynicism was preserving his stomach. He watched the young man twisting one end of his handsome handlebar mustache and stayed where he was.

"Hey, Rudolph," the young man coaxed softly. "It's Digby Bell. You know *me*. Come on, this is good stuff, man."

To prove his point, Digby bit off a piece of lettuce, chewed it slowly, and repeated his offer.

Finding nothing to fear in Digby's gentle voice, seeing no savagery in his clear, blue eyes, Rudolph stepped forward tentatively. He sniffed the lettuce with his nose, which had been painted red, and drew it out of Digby's hand.

"It's a hell of a life, Rudolph," Digby commiserated.

Rudolph chewed his lettuce and stayed close to the fence, permitting Digby to scratch under his chin and very gently run his finger over Rudolph's red nose.

They had met a month ago when by chance Digby's travels had taken him through the park. Hemmed in by crowds of curious shoppers, he

4

stayed to watch the tree-lighting ceremony and to hear the speech by the mayor. The length of the speech was unforgivable. And it seemed to Digby that when it was all added up, more time had been spent denouncing the mayor's enemies and critics than in restating the seasonal platitudes. But finally the switch was thrown and the oaks, the elms, and the maples had burst into clusters of red and blue stars. The crowd began to move about its business, sweeping Digby past the deer. That was when Digby saw Rudolph huddled at the back of his pen, his nose then fresh with iridescent paint. "Son of a bitch!" Digby had exclaimed. Behind him a chorus of city hall clerks sang "Silent Night," while the shrill hooting of traffic congestion in the nearby street swallowed up both sentiments.

Digby emptied his other pocket of lettuce. "I'll be back again before the big day, Rudolph," he said. Tucking the unsold painting under his arm, he hurried off. It was a long walk home and the first snow was beginning to fall.

If Christmas blossomed overnight and early downtown, it had been slow to spread to Digby's neighborhood, where people bought at the last minute and on credit, if at all. But nearing home Digby was cheered to find the weekend had finally raised a few trees. Here and there a window was bright with strings of lights lending grace to a dilapidated brick or brownstone house.

Digby slowed to a stop in front of a variety store which had Christmas trees stacked out front.

5

He shifted the burdensome picture under his left arm and stood considering the artificial woodland. With his free hand deep in his pocket, he fingered the icy change, feeling out quarters, dimes and nickels. There was a crumpled dollar bill, too, which brought his tally to something over two dollars. While Digby wondered if he could really spend the two dollars on a tree, and whether Blossom had any money left in their coffee can, the shop door opened and a squat woman came out, a coat thrown over her soiled apron. Her expression told Digby he was not a prime prospect.

"You want a tree?" she yelled, coming close to Digby. The wind was noisy and the snow was falling thicker.

"How much?" Digby asked.

"All prices," she yelled.

"How about that one?" Digby pointed to a large blue spruce.

The woman consulted a tag. "Six dollars," she said.

Digby shook his head. "All I've got is two dollars," he said, deciding not to prolong the business. Without Blossom along to haggle with the woman, the ritual wouldn't prove much fun anyway.

As it happened, she had quite a few two-dollar trees. It was a two-dollar-tree neighborhood. One look told Digby all the trees in this price range had problems, but he chose one quickly and paid the woman. "Merry Christmas!" he cried after her, but she fled into the shop without so much as a nod.

Digby hadn't moved far from the store when he had reason to wish he had put off the tree until tomorrow. The wind was against him and sent Digby — not a frail man by any means — staggering into the gutter when it caught the tree and the picture broadside. The snowflakes were no longer soft feathers or stars exploding at a touch, but sharp grains that stung Digby's face and fell into the neck of his parka, collecting in the hollows of his collarbone until they melted into cold trickles inching downward. By the time Digby reached the end of the block, he no longer felt his hands, and a crust of ice had formed over the top of his head. Nevertheless, his spirits were up. Buying the tree had changed the day and now he was anxious to get home. He stopped to get a painful breath of air and to look around. Up ahead he saw a fenced acre of asphalt which separated the House of the Holy Sojourners from the sidewalk. Half a block beyond was home.

It was the kitten that Digby saw first, making circles of footprints in the skin of snow forming over the sidewalk. It looked up at Digby and yowled, a scruffy bag of skin containing little else but its own bones. Then, screened by the high, chain-link fence, he saw a row of kneeling children, silent now, openly appraising him, their fingers poking through the fence toward the kitten to whom they had been offering hoarded scraps of cookies and candy bars. The kitten couldn't get in; they couldn't get out.

"It's a stray," a black child finally said, and

7

they waited to see what Digby would do with the information. Making soundless cries up at Digby, the kitten wove figure eights around Digby's old army boots.

But Digby knew what his own weaknesses were. He had already acquired two stray cats and a dog that had to be fed even if he went hungry. He shut his eyes against the scene. *Not* this *cat*, he said to himself. *This one has to be someone else's.*

"It ain't nobody's. Why don't you take it home?" another voice suggested, impatient with Digby's silence.

Digby looked up from the kitten to the spokesman. The boy's face mirrored the neighborhood's sorrows and his clothes, clean, mended and secondhand, made plain the economics of charity. This child was white, and a coldness having nothing to do with the temperature radiated from him. In the alabaster face there was no shred of innocence. Digby read in it the probability of his own refusal.

Digby said nothing, only lifted his feet from the kitten's invisible webs and started on, steeling himself for their benedictions. "Fink!" "Crud!" "Cheap bastard!" And worse things that hit his retreating back like knives.

A nun, who had been ringing a handbell summoning the children, now left the open doorway of the House. Being ignored had made her purposeful with anger and she made her way across the asphalt, a billowing black angel against the expanse of newly fallen snow. They would catch it now, thought Digby.

8

His stomach twisted, squeezing all hunger out of it. His good mood had vanished. Suddenly he became conscious that he was being followed on the other side of the fence and looking through he saw a girl. "Just take it for tonight," he heard her say. "We'll ask Sister if we can keep it," she promised.

Digby knew Sister would not take it in. He knew if he brought the animal home he would keep it. He wouldn't have the heart to take it somewhere only to have it put to sleep. He bowed his head into the storm and tried to go faster.

Man, you can't save every stray cat, he told himself. *The world's full of stray cats. Stray people, for that matter.* Digby's house was never empty now. He and Blossom hardly had a moment to be alone. Lost people and stray cats. There were times — and this was one of them — when it was harder to know who you were and where you were at, Digby reflected, than it was to be wandering the cold streets of the city. No, Digby decided immediately, this wasn't true, either. He wasn't lost and it was good not to be lost. If his manner of living was peculiar, he was perfectly aware of what he gave up by it and why he did so. Digby knew beauty and he knew peace since Blossom had come to him, and with her strength added to his own, it came as the natural thing for them to maintain a house where there was always room for someone who had a need.

As much as the kitten, the faces he left behind haunted him. He got only as far as the end of the wire fence when he turned around. With an exhilarating sense of relief, as though a terrible accident or some destructive turn of fate had been averted, he began to retrace his steps.

The children were being marched smartly single file across the acre of asphalt toward the stolid House of the Holy Sojourners. For a fearful moment, Digby thought the kitten had disappeared, but suddenly there it was, winding itself around his feet. He dropped the tree, scooped up the kitten, and tucked it into the deep pocket of his parka. His long fingers circled the bony animal, gently stroking its throat until he felt the vibration of a purr. Then he picked up the tree and ran ahead.

"Hey, little ones!" Digby yelled over the fence. "I got it! You hear me? I'm taking it home!"

Small heads turned in acknowledgment but no talking in ranks was allowed.

Digby ran the rest of the way home. He stopped in front of the house for a moment looking at the tubs of hardy chrysanthemums which Blossom and he had set out on either side of the doorway in the spring, and so he would not arrive home empty-handed, he broke off the season's last orange flower before climbing the steps.

Chapter 2

*B*ig Mohammed sucked deep on his cigar, pursed his lips and blew a long funnel of smoke against the plate-glass window of Pearl's Clam Box. Having thrown up his camouflage, he cleared a peephole in the fogged glass with a finger and put an eye to the spot which looked across the street at the House of the Holy Sojourners.

"Look at that white cat out there," he said, his voice like an echo from a deep well. "What's that white cat doing?"

Pearl glanced up from her sweeping. "You talking to me or yourself again?" she asked. She saw Big Mohammed concentrating on the street and leaned to peer through the glass panel of her door.

"That cat's been hanging around the neighborhood all week," she said. "I've swept him out of here more than once. It's a pretty little thing but I already have a cat."

Big Mohammed lifted his red velvet fez, resettled it, and directed a withering look in Pearl's direction. "I don't mean the *cat*," he said. "I mean that white boy trying to put down those black children behind the fence."

Pearl giggled. "Oh, that's Digby," she said, looking again. "He doesn't put anybody down. And anyway, half those children are white. That's your trouble, Big Mohammed, you only see the black half of anything."

Big Mohammed's eyes narrowed and his tiny prophet's beard dropped just a shade, enough to show a sly smile.

"Now, you're a black woman," he said. "You don't want me to think that white cat's a friend of yours."

"He is, matter of fact," Pearl said airily. "I take people like I find them. I wouldn't put a man down for his color."

"Now, you don't want me to think you're an Uncle *Tom*," Big Mohammed said, "because I am keeping a secret list of Uncle Toms. When the big day comes, if you find yourself on that list, you're in big trouble. I don't want to put you on our black boycott list."

"Would you really do that?" Pearl laughed. "Why, you big black bum, I'd consider myself lucky if I got fifteen cents for the coffee you drank, never mind no boycott. Why don't you get yourself a steady job, Dudley Harrison!"

"It's Big Mohammed," he corrected with solemn dignity. He drew himself up to his full height, which was impressive, but not so impressive as Pearl with a broom in her hands.

"Shame on you," Pearl scolded. "A big healthy man like you pussyfooting around the neighborhood like a hustler. Secret lists and secret meetings! Black revolutions and guns and bombs! You're about as dangerous as a hangnail. I swear, if I heard you sass back your landlady, I'd faint!"

"A lot you know," Big Mohammed hinted mysteriously. "Plans are laid. Big plans need big coordination. But I'm on schedule. Yes, ma'am!"

"How many in your army, General Mohammed?" Pearl inquired.

"That's classified information," Big Mohammed replied.

"Just you, is my guess," Pearl said.

Big Mohammed took this opinion with patience. "The day is coming when the citadels of white power will fall," he promised. "I don't give second chances to join up with me. And your black color won't help you if you're on our list." He winked extravagantly and put his eye back to the window.

"Well," Pearl considered, "it hasn't been any help up to now, and if you come to power, Big Mohammed, I don't suppose it will be any help to me then, either."

Big Mohammed lifted a hand for silence. "Look at that!" he whispered hoarsely. "He's put those black children's cat in his pocket! We can't even have ourselves a *cat* but what they take it away from us!" Big Mohammed quickly buttoned up

13

his trenchcoat and flipped up his collar. "I'll just put myself on his tail," he said. "I like to know where the enemy hides out."

Pearl shook her head. "Big Mohammed, you're something else," she sighed, watching him slip out into the storm.

Big Mohammed's hasty exit had not been designed to escape the tab, but since it turned out to be a nice diversionary action, he wished now he'd also had a sandwich. He often followed people just to keep in practice, just as he now scooped up a handful of snow and fashioned a hand grenade. He simulated pulling the pin, waited a tense few seconds, aimed it at a street light, and jumped into a doorway.

"Boom," he whispered aloud and stepped out to the disappointment of finding the street light still glowing. "Have to allow more for the wind," he reasoned. There was nothing wrong with his aim.

Skulking along close to the buildings, Big Mohammed followed thirty yards behind Digby and congratulated himself on his skill and technique. Only once was there difficulty and only then because he stepped into a pail some fool had left on his doorstep. But even then, Big Mohammed took advantage of his prone position on the sidewalk to wait out the ambush of machine-gun bullets whistling over his head and the Molotov cocktails bursting into fiery blossoms all around. Up ahead, unsuspecting Digby, clutching his picture and the tree, danced back and forth on the sidewalk, absorbed in keeping upright in the gale and accumu-

14

lating snow. Big Mohammed, judging the moment exactly right, jumped to his feet, felled a National Guard trooper or two armed with fixed bayonets, and once again set out after his quarry.

"I'm glad to know that cat's name," Big Mohammed thought, pleased at how cleverly he had wormed the information out of Pearl. "That cat goes on my list," he decided. He remembered with rising anger that last spring Digby's household had led the cleanup of the neighborhood's alleys only to deprive black children of the fun of pelting the rats with beer bottles. Since people like Digby began moving in, things were so quiet the police siren was hardly ever heard anymore. The other day when he threw a cigar wrapper on the sidewalk, an old woman had raised her window and called him a slob! The crowning insult was when Big Mohammed had come face to face with a Negro cop who suddenly appeared on the beat one morning. What kind of jazz was that, Big Mohammed had had to ask himself. Did anyone doubt now that black power was overdue? What further indignity was needed? Big Mohammed saw it all. Somehow it was Digby's doing, the advent of that big-mouthed policeman wanting to know if he was employed or not! Big Mohammed whipped his hand out of his pocket, folded his fingers to make a .38 pistol. Just when Digby was in proper range and Big Mohammed's arm was raised, Digby turned into a doorway flanked by two tubs of chrysanthemums and by the time Big Mohammed had sneaked sideways along the buildings to the house, he had disappeared altogether.

Big Mohammed stood before the house listening. From behind the blue-painted door came a faint, sweet sound of guitar-strumming, touching off a rage in Big Mohammed that welled up like fire in a roman candle. Like a sealed bottle, he trembled with it, stretched with it, gritted his teeth against the explosion coming. His eyes fell to Digby's tubs of chrysanthemums and, like a great hawk, his hand swooped down to yank up a plant by the roots. With a demoniac fury he flung it to the ground and proceeded to dance up and down on it until it was hardly more than a green smear on the beaten snow. Breathing heavily, spent and happy, he drew his head into his collar and looked suspiciously around the snow-blown street. Satisfied the raid on the enemy had been swift and telling and unobserved, he disappeared into the night, pausing only to fashion and throw a firebomb at the great round window of the church across from Digby's house. Allah would guide his aim.

Chapter 3

*T*he Reverend Sitwell stood motionless in what he euphemistically called his garden — a small square of beaten earth in front of St. Paul's, bounded by a cast-iron fence. It contained a wayside pulpit and also, at that moment, the minister himself. It was the time of the day on the day of the week that he changed the pulpit's message.

Sitwell had watched Big Mohammed's performance with curiosity, admiration even, but not alarm. His poor eyesight and the veil of snow between himself and Digby's steps allowed the old gentleman to think that what he witnessed was an innocent impromptu expression of primitive joy. Sitwell rather enjoyed a snowfall himself, but the emotion was more apt to come out in a sonnet. His desk was a pigsty of unfinished sonnets. Sitwell's image of his parish, insulated by the leaded windows of the parsonage, easily accommodated a Negro giant dancing the tarantella on the sidewalk during a blizzard. It was an offer from the giant to hold his box of letters while he worked that would have set him stuttering with surprise.

On his left arm Sitwell balanced a large flat box of plastic letters. Unfortunately, the box was filling up with snow, and the glass door of the pulpit, against which he had braced his back, flapped in the wind, jiggling his arm. Therefore, his progress was slow. It was nonsensical to be out-of-doors at all, but he was resisting the elements with good cheer. He knew himself to be a man of no great competence, but it was something, after all, to be dutiful to the pastoral routines he set for himself. After removing a word of last week's message, he sorted the letters into the box, then chose the letters for a word of the new message. In this way the wisdom of Jesus, for instance, might yield gradually to the insights of Sigmund Freud. Or vice versa.

St. Matthew had written and now Sitwell was painstakingly reproducing, "AND THEY SHALL CALL HIS NAME EMMANUEL, WHICH BEING INTERPRETED IS, GOD AMONG US."

God among us, Sitwell reiterated inwardly. Indeed he was, though the spirit was elusive in this neighborhood. Even at Christmas time. Sitwell was aware no one was more affected by the quotations he chose than himself, but he nevertheless sought them out from every conceivable source of inspiration and changed them each Monday with a punctuality even the present blizzard failed to alter. "God among us" was a strong article of faith here. He expected there would be skeptics. Now, Jean Jacques Rousseau was something else. "MAN IS BORN FREE, AND EVERYWHERE HE IS IN CHAINS," the pulpit had said for the past week. And working now to remove the quotation, Sitwell was struck again by its relevance to these times, as well as for Rousseau's. For all times. Was man then intended to be chained? Was it part of the eternal design? Sitwell didn't believe it. Not for a minute. But when he considered the poverty and ignorance around him, if it was a locksmith St. Paul's parish needed, then he was a man of sorry accomplishments.

As he worked, the wind sometimes picked letters from the old man's fingers, which alarmed him. Some letters were already in short supply, and though he could in a pinch substitute a Q or an upside-down U for an O, a Z for an S, he was conscious that too much of this sort of thing caused the sayings of Jesus or Havelock Ellis to look like Russian epigrams.

Sitwell's church, St. Paul's, was built of puddingstone and gave the impression of being held together by the webs of ivy that surrounded it. If it had any distinctive architectural feature, it was the great round stained-glass eye with which it looked across the street at Digby's house. This window had been a gift from a rich suburban parish dismantling its Romanesque building in favor of a complex of cantilevered concrete slabs which had struck Sitwell as uncomfortably similar to pieces of a crumpled airplane. As luck would have it, the denomination of the church and the Romanesque window had just fit St. Paul's. The Sunday supplement publicity had given Sitwell the impression that his humble, declining parish was receiving a medieval treasure in the enormous crate that was delivered, and it had not been until St. Paul's simple rose window had been replaced and the gift unveiled that the extent of his betrayal was known to him. In this neighborhood, which was largely black and altogether poor, here was a pink and golden-curled Jesus passing out loaves and green fishes to a multitude of Scandinavian sunbathers in an English seaside garden complete with hollyhocks. It was bad enough the neighborhood dubbed it "The Mayor Passing Out Welfare Checks," but it promised to beggar the parish with its insurance premiums. There was a poverty of supplies in his Sunday school and the organ was developing ominous wheezes. A small hurricane or sonic boom wouldn't be unwelcome when one considered what the insurance money could provide. Against this contingency, Sitwell kept the pieces of the rose window safely stored in the parsonage basement.

Suddenly, to Sitwell's consternation, a snowball the size of a meteor orbited into his field of vision. For the briefest joyful moment, his repressed wishes rose to the surface. Not breathing, he followed the snowball's arc until it splattered against the church, a yard to the left of the window.

"Damn!" the little man cursed under his breath and, in his agitation, nearly dropped his box of letters. He peeked around to find an empty street (or was there a black shadow flattened against a doorway?). He discreetly turned his back, hoping to see another snowball follow the first. Nothing followed except his own disappointment.

Oh Lord! he questioned, agonized, *why do you send me a mischief-maker and then give him such wretched aim? A child could have hit it from that distance. Why*, thought Sitwell, *even I could have hit it!*

The thought made him jump as though jabbed by a pin, and though he went back to work with a passion, it wouldn't leave him. "*E*mmanuel, Em*man*uel, Emmanu*el*," he repeated as he spelled out the letters. "Which being interpreted is . . ." But once the comma was in place, the urge to scan the street became irresistible. Empty! A wilderness! Blowing snow and soft glowing circles of street lamps giving no light. No one could see him. He had only to scoop up a handful of snow, make a hard ball of it, and send it across the night. The arrogant, pink fraud would lay in a thousand pieces on the choir loft floor.

Sitwell knew he was being tempted.

"And they shall call his name Emmanuel, which being interpreted is, God among us," he whispered aloud, his eyes shut in prayer. In the blackness, he felt himself sway in the wind and opened his eyes in time to see his box of letters tip its contents into the snow at his feet. The spell shattered, the hiss and whistle behind him once again was the snow and not the cooing of Satan in his ears. "Thank you, Lord," he said humbly.

He knelt awkwardly in the snow and began to pile handfuls of snow mixed with letters into the box. Tomorrow he would sort them out. Tomorrow he would finish. When he had retrieved all the letters he could, he knelt a moment longer though his knees and bare hands were numb from the cold. "I'm a foolish servant, Lord," he confessed softly. "Forgive me when I see Your will in my own ambitions."

He closed the pulpit's glass door and, assessing the weather around him, decided to leave the church lit and the door unlocked should some wandering soul need refuge for the night.

Inside, the snow-heaped box of letters was set by the study fire to melt, while the minister opened his evening bottle of sherry and drew the curtains against the storm.

Outside, the snow-blown passerby was left to ponder the combined wisdom of St. Matthew and Rousseau, which now read, "AND THEY SHALL CALL HIS NAME EMMANUEL, WHICH BEING INTERPRETED IS, EVERYWHERE HE IS IN CHAINS."

Chapter 4

Digby looked out the window across the street, following the black figure of Sitwell as he staggered against the force of the blizzard on his way to the church door. The old man's escape left the landscape without life, and it seemed to Digby that his perspective was suddenly inverted. It was the curtain of snow that hung stationary in space, while the landscape rushed past it with incredible speed, headlong, on and on. He knew behind him was the nearly bare room and he could hear Blossom talking nonsense to the kitten. From the room next door came guitar chords, bright sharp sounds lingering on his ear as fireworks linger in the eye after the sparks have died. Everyone, everywhere, Digby thought, streaking through the universe, while the snow hung cold, motionless, sparkling in the air.

Blossom lay on their bed. Though neatly made,

it was like everything else in the house, simplified to its essence, in this case a mattress on the floor. The kitten was spread over the swollen mound of her belly, its eyes shut, its paws kneading her breasts in an ecstacy of warmth and security.

"What shall we name it, Digby?" she asked.

Digby turned away from the window and looked down on them thoughtfully. "Emmanuel," he said.

A smile played over Blossom's lips at the thought.

"Why Emmanuel?" she asked.

"A sign from Big Daddy," Digby replied soberly. " 'And they shall call his name Emmanuel, which being interpreted' . . ."

"Is what?" inquired Blossom, looking up.

Digby had recognized the tag end of Rousseau. "It means," he smiled, "another mouth to feed."

"Well, let's see if you *are* an Emmanuel," Blossom said, and shifting the kitten, she peered under its tail. "Emmanuel you are," she pronounced.

Digby was strongly moved by the sight of Blossom with the kitten. He saw a gentleness in Blossom's hands stroking the bony animal. Her natural beauty aside, she possessed a grace of temperament that healed the fractures of his days. Her pregnancy, he thought, had made her luminous, a Renaissance figure touched here and there with gilt.

"I'm a trouble to you, aren't I, Digby?" Blossom said, mistaking Digby's expression for concern.

Digby's face opened in shock. "My salvation, baby, not my trouble."

He left the window and settled on the mattress beside her, letting his hand rest on her abdomen beside the kitten. But even as he laughed softly, feeling the child kick, Blossom saw weariness behind his eyes. She worried that somehow the child would be the undoing of its father, that Digby would now feel an obligation to run to the market-place and take on the veneers of respectability. She had put off telling him of the child, had not told him at all, in fact. What became obvious to the homeless that passed through their derelict house somehow escaped Digby's attention until one night when they held each other in love, Digby had found himself arched so high over her that no other explanation was necessary.

"Blossom . . . ?" she had heard him ask warily in the darkness.

"Yes, Digby, that's what it is," Blossom had sighed.

"Hey, how about *that!*" he had replied, and though he had from that moment given every evidence of enthusiasm, Blossom was afraid that his present melancholy had its origin in that moment.

"You can't say I'm not a good provider," Digby said, scratching the kitten's chin.

"A good provider provides what's needed," Blossom said, ignoring his sarcasm. "You've always done that."

"You *needed* another cat," he laughed.

"I'll always need another cat," she said. "And

the tree. We needed a tree and you provided a tree."

The tree now leaned against the corner with its trunk in a pan of water. "It's pretty lopsided," he observed.

"So am I," said Blossom.

The idle strumming of the guitar in the next room fell into the familiar pattern of a Spanish folk dance Digby had heard a hundred times before.

"Happy bought himself a new E-string," Digby said, listening.

"I gave him the money out of the coffee can," Blossom said. "In fact, I made him take it."

"Sure," Digby agreed. "Is there much left in the can?" he forced himself to ask.

"We'll manage," Blossom said.

Digby got up from the floor and picked up the returned canvas. He hung it carefully on a nail in the wall and stood peeling away the last few shreds of wet newspaper.

"I guess tomorrow I'll get myself some kind of little job for the holidays," he said matter-of-factly. "Nothing too much. You know what I mean? Something to put a little bread on the table."

Blossom overlooked the suggestion and asked, "What excuse did she give you?"

Digby seemed not to have heard. "It's a good portrait," he said, studying the picture.

"Why wouldn't she take it?" Blossom insisted. "A commission is a commission, isn't it?"

Digby shrugged. "She doesn't see herself this

way, I guess. She said I made her look hard, ugly. Like a dummy in a store window."

Digby was not of the slap and dribble school. He took infinite pains with his paintings which, when finished, were thick with paint and trembling with life. He never did still lifes, seldom did landscapes. It was the landscapes of the soul on which Digby labored. He painted faces rich with life and sometimes faces barren as sand. Like a geologist, he probed beneath the planes and surfaces of his subjects' faces and painted what he found there, treasure or basalt. It was no accident that light glittered only from the surfaces of the eyes of the lady on the wall.

Still, as a piece of work, Digby was satisfied with it. "I'll put it in the next League show," he decided.

When singing voices joined the guitar, Digby's head cocked quizzically to the doorway. "Who's the girl in there singing with Martha?" he asked.

"Someone Martha found today," Blossom replied, wishing she had thought to mention it before.

"What's she like?" Digby asked.

"She's young. Very quiet."

"Did she look clean to you?"

"I got a quick look in her bag. Nothing there," Blossom said. "She doesn't say anything about herself and I didn't ask."

"I'll ask," Digby said. "If she's not clean, she can only stay the night."

Digby asked nothing of his guests, and seldom

27

got anything. But about one thing he was unequivocal. On the stair landing was a large, carefully lettered sign reading: ABSOLUTELY NO POT, HORSE, SPEED, ET CETERA WILL BE BROUGHT INTO THIS HOUSE! NOTHING, MAN, UNLESS YOU HAVE A BONA FIDE PRESCRIPTION TO SHOW. NO SECOND CHANCES. Digby meant it, and while it saddened him to do so, the rare violator quickly found himself and his belongings, if he had any, hustled out onto the sidewalk.

A doleful black and tan hound beside the stove unwound himself, yawned, and padded slowly over to Blossom, his tail describing large circles as he stood by her, one paw resting on her shoulder. Two sleek cats rose from the foot of the mattress, stretched, and with the dog, began a kind of contradance around Blossom.

"Our good friend, Picasso, is hungry," Blossom said, sitting up with difficulty. "Everybody's hungry. Even Emmanuel."

"Man, ain't *that* the truth," Digby said. "Hungry for food, hungry for love, hungry for a kind word. But we're all warm. That's something. We run a warm house, Blossom."

Not long ago Digby had sealed the loose window sashes with wide masking tape, and without these drafts the two habitable rooms on the second floor were kept extravagantly warm. The first floor of the house was not usable. Some of the ceilings had fallen and the windows were boarded up with plywood. The third floor was impossible to heat.

The house, along with its neighbors on either side, was scheduled for demolition sometime in the future, something that caused Digby little concern. His present way of life didn't allow for the collection of possessions. Those he had had legs of their own with which to make a hasty exit when the time came. Digby had given hospitality freely and at various times his guests, in gratitude, had managed to connect the gas, electricity and water. In this room he and Blossom shared, an ancient stove had been made to partially function, and in each of the two second floor rooms one electric light could be counted on to work. How these miracles came to pass, Digby didn't know. All he knew was no gas or electric bill ever arrived.

When Blossom got up to prepare the evening meal, Digby stretched out on the mattress, cushioning his head with his arms. He was silent so long, Blossom thought he was sleeping, but when she glanced over, she found him frowning, his eyes focused intently on the ceiling over his head.

"What do you see up there?" she questioned softly.

"Cracks," he answered promptly. "Cracks making a wire fence. Behind the fence, I see faces. All kinds of little faces in the shadows of that fence, Especially one cold, white face like alabaster. With eyes so sharp they draw blood."

The tone of his voice disturbed Blossom. She turned back to the beef stew which bubbled on the stove, and worked at its flavor with her spices, picking things up and putting them down with deliberate care as though there were sickness in the house.

"Did you ever notice the House of the Holy Sojourners?" Digby asked, breaking a long silence. "I mean really take a good look at it."

"I notice it sometimes. Not like you do, I guess," Blossom replied.

"Stop and look through the fence next time," Digby said. "Watch them at play, those hard, wise faces. And those eyes! They don't blink at anything. They already know everything there is to know." He sighed and after a while asked irritably, "Why do I break up over kids? I had a good childhood."

"You're an artist," Blossom smiled. "You're part child."

"I have to mind my own business," he concluded. "Every good impulse has another cat tied to it."

"Digby, you can't take in every child behind every fence," Blossom said sensibly.

"I know," Digby said, but it seemed to Blossom that before he agreed, he weighed the possibility.

The smell of Blossom's heating stew spread through the second floor. The music in the next room stopped with a flourish of chords and Digby's household convened for its evening meal.

The room had only one table, too small to eat on, and no chairs at all, so they were accustomed to sitting or reclining in a circle on the floor.

Martha, whose speech like her person was innocent of frills, presented the stranger to Digby with a simple "Digby, this is Cleo."

Digby nodded, said "Hello," and smiled in a way meant to be friendly. But while he waited for the food to circle around to him, he coolly appraised the girl. Blossom had been right. She was young. Barely sixteen, if that. If she were a runaway, her age could prove a liability. And with Blossom so close to delivery, Digby was reluctant to take on liabilities.

Digby's eyes left the girl and moved partway around the circle to Happy. The thin young man was bent over the plate resting on his lap. Digby studied the fine curly black hair he had never done on canvas to his satisfaction, though Happy posed for hours, uncomplaining, with his guitar cradled in his lap. Digby considered his best portrait was of Happy, but in it, it was Happy's hands that were alive, not the dark-toned, somber face. He watched Happy now picking disinterestedly at his food, and asked casually, "You OK, Happy?"

Happy looked up quickly and replied, "I'm OK, Dig."

Was he? Digby wondered. It was hard to tell. Except for Happy's fine tenor singing voice, he was virtually mute. In the months he had stayed with them, Digby had learned to respect Happy's private world. The boy was stable unless pressured, helpful to Blossom, and had no bad habits that Digby and Blossom could detect, except a tendency to sometimes disappear for a few days, after which Blossom would find several ten-dollar bills in the coffee can. Where he went or how he came by the money was his own secret. Digby fully expected Happy would one day unfold, but it would happen without pressure, like a flower in its season. In the meantime, he was glad to sing. But like a bird whose song came from deep in the thicket.

"I have eight dollars for the coffee can," Martha announced, obviously pleased with herself. "I'd have had more except I had to go to a demonstration at the Federal Building. Later a cop chased me off the corner which didn't help. Then, when I found a new corner, the snow made my papers soggy. Try selling a soggy *Aquarius* to a wet stockbroker sometime."

"What do they get for *Aquarius* now?" Digby asked, not really interested.

"It's still thirty-five cents," Martha replied.

"Too much for a lot of dirty classifieds and half-baked ideas. What do *you* get?"

"A nickel."

Digby made a grunt of disapproval which was a dismissal both of the underground newspaper and the subculture that had grown up around it. Digby was a creative man, and though he could have listed many people he admired — other creative people, mostly — he worshiped no one, followed no movement.

"Guess who's got a full-page, three-color ad on the back page?" Martha asked, not put off by Digby.

"It has to be our good friend, Bernard," Digby replied. "It's on my mind to put a bronze plaque on the floor right under your tail where he used to sit."

Martha looked up at Digby curiously and pushed her steel-rimmed glasses up the bridge of her thin nose. "Want to see the ad?"

"No."

"I thought you liked Bernard."

"Bernard's all right," Digby said, but in truth, he was hurt that Bernard had taken so much and then had made his sudden rise without a single backward glance at old friends.

"I'm working on a Christmas carol," Happy announced unexpectedly, and momentarily everyone stopped chewing.

"That's great!" Digby said. "Let's hear it."

"It's not finished," Happy said apologetically and retreated once again behind his wall of silence.

During the meal, Martha chattered about her day. If her exterior was plain as the weathered stone of St. Paul's, inside she was a furnace of outrage against the ways of the world. Digby was sure if Martha wasn't making the world better, she was certainly making it more uncomfortable. But Digby was preoccupied and only half-listened until her story touched on finding Cleo. The girl disturbed Digby. Apart from the puzzling familiarity, there was an air of neglect about her as though she had lost or never achieved a sense of self. Her natural prettiness that might have blossomed into beauty had it been touched by spirit and animation, some sense of worth, seemed unalive, ill fitting and not her style.

When the meal was finished, Digby asked the girl to go with him into the other room.

"Sit down," Digby said kindly, and shut the door behind them. Seeing her confusion at there being no place to sit, he indicated the center one of three mattresses and tried to put her at ease. "The better hotels," he smiled, "they have chairs."

She sat obediently, folded her hands, and watched Digby run his hands over the window casings feeling for drafts. Sheets of snow blew against the windows and Digby congratulated himself for having spent an afternoon sealing the house.

Finally he knelt in front of the girl. "Lift your head up toward the light," he said gently. "Don't be nervous. I only want to see the pupils of your eyes."

Fine eyes, Digby thought. *Clear. A deep blue, almost black. Normal-sized pupils.*

"Good," he said. "Now let me see your arms. Push your sweater sleeves up."

As she did so he could see the skin was smooth and unmarked.

"You pass," he said, standing up. "Congratulations. If you smoke, stick to the standard brands."

Cleo smiled for the first time. "Did you think I was a junkie?"

He shrugged. "I had to know. People don't always believe my sign downstairs. It can make a lot of trouble for all of us," he explained. "Besides, I have a thing about drugs," he continued in a tone that was suddenly passionate for all its quiet control. "They don't give perception, they take it away. You know what I mean? I *have* to see. I *have* to feel. Sometimes it makes me feel beautiful. Sometimes it tears me up. Whatever it does to me, it comes from the inside out. I don't swallow it and I don't jab it in my arm. All I have is my paints, my brushes, and my insides. And I've worked for my insides. That's how I like it." He relaxed and grinned sheepishly. "How old are you?"

"Seventeen."

"Maybe sixteen?" he corrected.

"Seventeen. Almost eighteen."

"OK," he laughed.

"Nobody's looking for me, if that's what you think."

"You're sure?"

"I know," she said simply.

"Tomorrow I could take you to some people who would help you get home," he said. "It's no sweat. They're good people. No forms to make out in triplicate and all that crap." He raised a hand against her objections. "Don't say no, yet. Think about it." He leaned against the wall and surveyed this half of his kingdom with a wry smile. "Take a look around you," he said. "It's not much, and you should understand that I *know* why I'm here and Blossom knows why she's here. I skip some things so I can have other things. I bargain with life for

35

what I need most. I live plain, but I dream fancy. But you're not me. You're a different person. You have to think what *you* need."

"I need a place to stay, and I have nothing to give you," she said with an honesty Digby respected. "Martha said maybe you'd let me stay for a while, but she didn't promise."

Digby looked down on her and wondered again what was so familiar about her.

Cleo looked up at him to find his forehead wrinkled with concentration.

"I'd try to help out," she offered shyly. "I'd help Blossom."

"Stay," he said finally, and resting his hands lightly on her shoulders, added, "what's more, you're welcome."

Later, all around the darkened house the wind whistled and beat snow against its walls. In the dark, Digby lay on his mattress beside Blossom with his arms cushioning his head, his eyes open, his ears hearing wailing voices in the tumult of the storm outside. The smell of the Christmas tree lay over the room like incense. Blossom, not comfortable in any position, lay an arm across his chest and murmured sleepily. "The house is so warm, Digby."

Long after Blossom had drifted into sleep, Digby solved his puzzle and knew that Cleo's familiarity was no more than the same lonely despair he had seen in the children behind the fence.

"The house is so warm, Digby," he whispered to the silent room, "why is the world so cold?"

Chapter 5

St. Paul's abounded in birds. In spring they nested in the eaves or where the tough ropes of ivy branched, and in winter they took shelter in the crannies of carved stone, depending for food on the largesse of St. Paul's rector. Digby had just finished shoveling his own walk when he saw Sitwell appear with a snow shovel in one hand and a bag of crumbs in the other which he began sprinkling over the snow in the square of iron fencing. By the time Sitwell had wallowed through the drifts to the curb, the air around his wayside pulpit teemed with a flock of quarreling sparrows.

Crossing the street, Digby pole-vaulted on his shovel over the high ridge of snow the plow had left, landing in front of the minister, much to the good man's surprise.

"I'll help you do your walk," Digby offered.

Sitwell looked at Digby, whose shoveling had

left him the image of youthful vigor and good health. Digby looked at Sitwell, who had turned a bit blue from the cold, a color which had a regrettable tendency to accentuate the rum blossoms in his cheeks. The two men stared into each other's faces as curiously as two keyholes looking into one another.

How white his teeth are, thought Sitwell. *And how tall he is close up. His clothes are too small for him but I see they are clean and mended. He's always frightened me but here he stands with the most disarming of smiles. What are your motives, my son? Are they deeper than kindness to an old man? Well, we shall see.*

He drinks too much, thought Digby. *And he's too old to shovel snow. It's an old face but it's a good face. A rich face. What's behind those bright eyes of yours, little preacher? Are they looking for my virtues or my faults?*

"It's a neighborly offer," Sitwell said aloud. "And a welcome one, might I add."

"But not for money, understand," Digby clarified.

"For my thanks, then," Sitwell agreed, thankful he had not immediately launched into bargaining.

They pulled off their gloves, shook hands, and completed the simple amenities that might lead to friendship, each with an inner consciousness that curiosity was playing its part in the undertaking.

Neither was a hurrier by temperament and Sitwell felt inclined to chat, so the path to the church door grew slowly. "We might make it narrower," Sitwell observed, surveying the generous size of their effort. "It won't get much traffic, you know."

Digby leaned against his shovel and considered the church and the adjacent parsonage. "It makes the church look better," he said. "A narrow path louses up the lines of the doorway, ruins the whole perspective."

"But of course," Sitwell cried. "You're a painter. I see you pass sometimes with canvases under your arm."

The bright sun on the crystalline whiteness of the snow pleased Digby enormously. Burning his energies carving out blocks of snow, tossing them high in the air, gave him a feeling that was near sensuality. "Man, I go out with them," he laughed, "and I come home with them!"

"The artist has a hard lot, but you must stick to it, Digby," Sitwell said. "Every form of labor has its discouragements. Even mine. That I have a church at all, I think, depends on the slender thread of the bishop's mercy."

"No money?" Digby asked.

"Worse than that. No congregation," the old man replied sadly. "I lack the apostolic gift. When I came here to St. Paul's, shortly after the Flood," he smiled, "things went well. I was busy enough to have an assistant. But time never leaves man or his works alone. The neighborhood even then was beginning a transition. Would you believe it, Digby, forty years ago the commonest sight in the morning on this street was hired girls out

39

sweeping the steps? But then my flock of old white sheep fled before the immigrants and the immigrants before the black people. Now the black sheep need a better shepherd than I am. They don't come to St. Paul's, many of them. Not to excuse my shortcomings," he continued, "but I should have married. I know myself to be a lonely old man and out of touch. Life attracts life. A good woman would have created a warmth and busyness around this old building. A magnet to draw others across the threshold."

"A woman is the center of everything," Digby agreed.

"Your wife is lovely," Sitwell said. "We have said hello to one another once or twice."

Digby's face went momentarily blank. "Not my wife," he said, strangely disturbed by the correction. "My . . ." For a moment he grasped for a word and found nothing satisfactory. "I just love her," he explained. "You know what I mean?"

"Yes, I think so," the old man replied kindly. "Well, perhaps not, really, but allow me to think I do."

A sudden flash of inspiration straightened Digby up on his shovel. "Would you like a cat?" he asked. "To keep you company?"

"A cat?" Sitwell repeated, surprised.

"A kitten," Digby said hopefully. "A white kitten."

"It's an idea I've never considered," Sitwell said.

His first thought was to accept. He was fond of cats. A second thought, following hard on the first, was that Mrs. Jenks, his housekeeper, would disapprove. But the thought of a cat curled up by his study fire was attractive.

"It's an affectionate cat," Digby argued. "It's been hanging around the orphanage. The kids last night bugged me to take it home out of the snow. I've already got two cats and a hound. I mean, I'll keep it, but I thought you might like it. You know, for company."

Sitwell brushed Mrs. Jenks aside and said, "Yes, I *will* take it! How different today is from yesterday," he chuckled. "I am becoming a family man!"

"Great!" Digby cried. "And sometime when you go by, tell those kids you're keeping the cat. Just yell it over the fence. You could tell by their faces they didn't want to give it away. They just didn't have any choice."

"No choice at all," Sitwell repeated and lapsed thoughtful. "I'll make a point of letting them know," he said finally. "I know those children, Digby. They're always on my mind in this season devoted to a Child, and so ostensibly *for* children. But for other children, not for them."

"They've kind of been on my mind, too," Digby said.

"I used to know the House of the Holy Sojourners very well," Sitwell reminisced. "I know the good Sisters there do what they can, but no one

41

pretends it is enough. The Mother Superior who used to be there and I became good friends. She sometimes took tea with me on a Sunday afternoon, bringing another Sister with her, of course, and together we considered the problems of her ministry. She felt it was the restoration of some measure of innocence to these unfortunates which was the crux of the matter, for she believed, and I concur, some innocence is required in every decent man." Sitwell looked toward the middle of the block where the wire fencing was visible, though not the House itself. "She was a good woman," he said. "On Christmas she would send a Sister down with a bottle of sherry for me, an indication of her kindness, and also," he smiled, "her understanding. She was very old even then. Unfortunately, she became quite dotty and had to be sent away. All this was some years ago. I don't know the new Mother Superior."

When at last their efforts brought their shovels scraping against the wide doorstep of St. Paul's, they straightened up and Sitwell looked up at the wooden doorway.

"I've hardly done anything about Christmas, yet," Sitwell said. "Not even a wreath on the door. Now it's time to brighten up a bit. I'd like to cover that awful window with evergreen boughs," he suggested wistfully. "Let me borrow your esthetic sense, Digby. What do you suggest to cheer up the building, to put it in a festive mood? Inexpensively," he added.

Digby's eyes scanned the front of the church and in a flash it came to him. "Children," he said, almost inaudibly, and then repeated it. "Children, man!"

Sitwell, puzzled, looked at his doorway again and felt Digby's hand grasp his shoulder. "I'm serious," he said. "Fill the place with children! Bring in those kids from the orphanage! The neighborhood kids!"

"A kind of party, you mean?" Sitwell asked, unnerved by the thought.

"Not a party," Digby cried. "A happening, man! Lights! Music! Joyful noises!"

"A candlelight procession," the old man thought aloud, warming to the idea. "Carols! A tree!"

"You want the black sheep in your church?" Digby said. "Hell, man, let's fill it!"

"A community celebration! For anyone who will come," Sitwell said, trembling both with excitement and dread.

They impatiently pushed open the door of the church and entered the dark aromatic gloom of the place, Sitwell already seeing it filled with a congregation.

Much could be done, Digby saw. The pews were screwed to the floor and could be moved if necessary. The ceilings were high and plain white plaster, which would take projections if he could get some. The overhead choir loft on the street end had possibilities. Digby immediately thought of Bernard.

"But Digby, we have no money," Sitwell suddenly exclaimed, already teetering on the edge of disappointment.

"Hell, money would get in the way," Digby said. "I've something better. I've got Bernard!"

Chapter 6

Digby paused at home only long enough to pilfer the coffee can of some money and to collect a pad of watercolor paper, a few brushes, and a half-dozen small jars of poster paints. While Blossom put together a peanut butter sandwich for him, Digby recounted for her the details of the happening as he, at this point, knew them.

By noon he had covered most of the grocery stores in the neighborhood with varying degrees of success. His requests were modest — boxes of cookies, candy, gallon jugs of cider and bottles of Coke — and in all but one shop he got at least some of what he hoped for, if not all. He carefully listed each shop and what it pledged so that on the following Saturday someone — probably himself — could pick up the donations. In each shop he dashed off a poster to be tacked up somewhere and wished everyone a merry Christmas before he left.

His last stop in the neighborhood before the long walk downtown was at Pearl's Clam Box, where he squandered fifteen cents on a cup of coffee and ate his peanut butter sandwich.

"Why, Digby, I'd be glad to contribute," Pearl said. "I'll make up six dozen doughnuts. And I'll roll some in green sugar and some in red."

"That's a lot, Pearl," Digby said gratefully. "Maybe you don't have to do so much."

Pearl waved him away. "Shoot, it's an hour of my time. Why, I turn out doughnuts faster than I breathe. I put my children through college on my doughnuts. The clams and French fries keep me afloat and what I need extra comes from doughnuts. Did your wife deliver yet? Last time she went by she looked due and then some."

Digby frowned into his coffee and resisted the impulse to correct her. "Not yet," he said.

"Well, you tell her to start carrying a laundry basket around with her when she goes out, just in case," Pearl laughed.

When Digby left, Pearl taped the small poster to her window and turned to see a puff of smoke appear over the top of the last booth in the corner, followed by a red fez.

"Now, what do you suppose that cat's got up his sleeve this time," Big Mohammed wondered aloud.

"It's not what's up his sleeve bothers me, Dudley Harrison," Pearl said. "It's what's on your mind."

Big Mohammed smiled mysteriously, winked at Pearl and said, "I'll tell you, baby. It's sabotage. Sa-bo-tage!"

On his long walk downtown, Digby thought pleasantly ahead to seeing Bernard again. It wasn't hard to find him. His Vesuvius Lighting Company, Inc., had grown large enough to occupy the abandoned Henry David Thoreau Grammar School, and its most profitable subsidiary, the Aurora Borealis — a kind of psychedelic discotheque — occupied on Friday and Saturday night what had once been the assembly hall. Under its present tenant, the grim Victorian building had shucked off its academic past and entered show business at an age when the laws of probability predicted it should collapse into a heap of cheap brick and plaster. Though its infirmities made it unsafe for slum children — and that, Digby knew, was very unsafe indeed — it had not been found so unsafe that college students couldn't crowd in to wiggle to the strains of rock, ogle the go-go dancers, and be blinded by the light shows Digby's friend Bernard produced. From penniless, humble beginnings as a guest in Digby's extra room, Bernard had risen to an entrepreneur of illusion, and the feelings his extravaganzas did not produce in his paying customers, with his tribal music, exploding lights, still and moving projections, glittering beads between the thighs of go-go girls, was not to be had except by putting a finger to the third

47

rail of the subway which brought them in from the suburbs. Digby had never seen one. Tickets were expensive and Bernard did not give passes to friends out of policy since, as he explained, he had so *many* of them.

It had been a good while since Digby had seen Bernard, though he had watched Vesuvius and Aurora Borealis ads in the underground newspapers and magazines grow from postage-stamp size to their present full-page color spreads. Even so, he wasn't prepared to find such an affluent Bernard, comfortably settled in a Saarinen chair and resplendent in a white linen jumpsuit, a psychedelic volcano embroidered on the chest.

"Man, you've made it! It's Wonderland!" Digby said, easing himself into a chair which was not, like Bernard's, a genuine Saarinen, a fact Digby only later found relevant.

"I *have* done well," Bernard said with satisfaction and leaned back in his chair, away from the red Formica desk. "I eat well, I sleep well, I pay cash." A pretty blond walked in, but seeing Bernard's visitor, hastily excused herself. "I play with pretty toys," Bernard smiled.

"No more mattresses on the floor, Bernard," Digby said.

"Water beds, baby, all the way. King size."

"Man, that hair!" Digby said. He found Bernard's golden shoulder-length hair the hardest of all to believe.

Bernard glanced cautiously at the doorway and giggled. "It's a wig, Dig." To prove it he lifted it up and then carefully replaced it. "People expect me to be weird. So I am," he explained. "It's good business and I can take it off my taxes. But you! You always did look like a leftover Beatle. Let your hair grow, man, and you'll sell pictures like mad."

"It would drag in the paint," Digby replied.

"Blossom still with you?" asked Bernard.

"More than ever."

Bernard suddenly leaned forward. "She wouldn't like a job, would she? I've got a dozen units rented out New Year's Eve and I'm running out of go-go girls."

"She wouldn't be interested," Digby said.

"Man, that girl's got a beautiful tail," Bernard sighed. "She could do it. You just wiggle your rump towards the paying customers. Is that so hard to do?"

Digby bristled inside at the idea but he made a thin laugh. "You wouldn't want her," he said, and held his arms out to make a bow over his stomach.

"God!" Bernard groaned. "How soon?"

"Any minute."

"God, what a lousy break, Dig!"

"Oh no," Digby corrected hastily. "It's great. I want it. We both want it. I mean, what the hell," he shrugged. "I love kids."

"Sick! You're sick!" Bernard cried. "But then, you always were."

"I guess," Digby agreed. "Bernard, I didn't just come by to visit. I have a favor to ask."

"Oh, Dig, baby!" Bernard cried, shutting his eyes and covering his ears with his hands. "Don't ask me for a job. *Please* don't ask me for a job!"

"No, I didn't come for a job," Digby said.

"Don't ask me for money! I *know* you're up against it, but *everybody's* up against it. All this is eyewash, Dig. Eyewash! I haven't got a dime. *Please* don't put the bite on me!"

"I don't want your money, Bernard," Digby said.

Bernard opened his eyes and uncovered his ears. "Ask me anything," he said.

Summoning what courage remained after this brief exchange, Digby said, "I'm working up this kind of happening thing for Saturday night . . ."

"Now you're hitting where I live, Dig. Happenings *are* Vesuvius Lighting, Inc.," Bernard said with a businesslike tone. "Give me the details. Where is it going to be and how much have they got to spend?"

"It's in a church, the one across from me," Digby replied. "And we don't have any money to spend."

Bernard's lips compressed and his fingers twisted little ringlets in his hair; his brow furrowed with deep thought. Finally he pulled a clipboard from the desk and flipped through its pages. "Here's just the thing," he announced. "Whoops, sorry, that's already committed to the Knights of Columbus that night. Well, here's . . . no, that's got to go to the Temple Shalom. Wrong color setup anyway. You'd want, let's see . . ."

"Greens and reds and stars," said Digby with a heavy heart.

Bernard curled a strand of hair behind his ear and sighed. "God, Dig, you wouldn't believe how popular light shows are these days. Everybody wants one," he apologized. "I don't have a thing free Saturday night. Not a forty-watt bulb."

Bernard looked up into Digby's eyes and immediately found much to interest him on the ceiling and the floor.

"Bernard, I fed you and I housed you for months," he heard Digby say. "I listened to you tell how bad the world treated you until I wanted to stuff cotton in my ears. I scraped up half the money to put together the first strobe light you played with." His voice was low and controlled but, nevertheless, Bernard found himself leaning away from the desk where Digby's hands gripped the edge. "I've never asked you for anything or wanted anything," Digby continued. "But if you take, man, you've got to give. I *want* those lights for orphan kids and slum kids! I want one, just one night of their lives to open up with surprise and joy. I want their childhood to be at least one night long. You have something, Bernard. Just think, man!"

For some seconds, Bernard's fingers drummed silently on the desktop. "Wait, I *do* have something," he decided suddenly. "As a matter of fact, it's the first lighting outfit I ever put together for Aurora Borealis. I'm goddamned sentimental about it. I've been planning to put it in a glass case in the lobby. Part of it is the very strobe you mentioned. Of course," he said regretfully, "it's not exactly in working order. You'd have to do some rewiring, I think. But you can do *that*. There may be some controls and timers missing, but you *take* it, Digby, with my blessings. Take it home, spread out the components, see what you can do with it."

"You mean," Digby said, "you'll let me take the lights, fix them so they work, use them one night, and then bring them back to you."

Bernard leaned back in his chair and looked reproachfully at Digby. "Baby," he smiled sadly, "that's no way to put it. After all, it's not *me* putting the bite on *you*."

Digby rose slowly from the imitation Saarinen chair. He put his hands firmly on the red desk and leaned far over, as close to Bernard as possible. "Go get me your fucking lights!" he whispered.

When Digby had dragged the lighting equipment from the cab and piled it in the cold, darkened church, he stepped across to the parsonage where lights burned, and rang the bell.

Sitwell was glowing with excitement. "Digby, what a stroke of luck we've had!" he exclaimed. "Come in, my boy, come into the study." His voice dropped to secrecy. "How quickly the community has responded! Come and see!"

Digby followed Sitwell down a dark passage which opened up into a warm book-lined study where a roaring fire threw three black shadows leaping up the walls.

"Hearing of our plans, a member of the black

community has come forward to join our enterprise," he announced to Digby in a formal way. "Digby, I should like you to meet Mr. Dudley Harrison. Mr. Harrison, Mr. Digby Bell."

Big Mohammed rose slowly from the sofa and, grinning widely, crushed Digby's hand. "Charmed, I'm sure," he said with his deep, beautiful voice.

"I was just opening a bottle of Bristol Cream," Sitwell said, proving it with the squeaky pop of a cork. "It's awfully good sherry, not at all what I usually drink. I think the moment calls for a toast, don't you?" He handed around three fragile glasses and smiled at Digby and Big Mohammed. They raised their glasses. "Peace on earth," Sitwell toasted. "Good will toward all men."

All three put glass to mouth and, as they did so, looked down into the brown wine which seemed to flicker from its depths with the warmth and light of the fire. In the peculiar alchemy of the moment, Sitwell dreamed of recreating the Fezziwigs' Christmas. Digby saw exploding stars, and Mr. Harrison weighed the possibilities of bombs. Stink, or smoke? Or maybe both?

Chapter 7

*D*igby woke early the next morning pleased to see the light of the rising sun through the windows was muted by thick coatings of frost flowers. Without disturbing Blossom, he slipped into his clothes and turned on all the stove's burners. With the room warming up, he closed the door to the other room so that no one would be awakened. With a kind of nervous, happy anticipation, he sat cross-legged against the stove, watching Blossom sleeping, until the coffee perked.

"Busy day ahead, baby," he said, softly stroking Blossom's cheek until her eyes fluttered open. "That's it, wake up with a smile," he crooned. "Come and see what the ghost of Aubrey Beardsley painted on our windows last night."

Blossom held the warm coffee mug against her cheek and shut her eyes again. "Don't go to sleep," Digby said. "Lots to do today. We have to get us a blood test." Blossom's eyes snapped open and she struggled to a sitting position. "You have to have a blood test to get married," he explained, completely unnerved by the flood of tears that welled up in Blossom's eyes.

"I knew all along it would come to this," she wailed. "Oh, Digby, I knew it couldn't last."

Digby folded her into his arms and kissed her wet face. "Come on, baby. Don't cry. Don't you want to marry me?"

"It's the beginning of the end," she sobbed. "Now you'll run out and get some job you don't want. You'll fall into the pit. All I want is for my baby's father to be a free man, not a slave!"

"Listen, Blossom," Digby said gently. "A man has to protect his child. If something happened to you, what would happen to the little one? You think they'd let me have it? Maybe, maybe not. Would you want our baby to go to some orphanage?"

The thought sobered Blossom and she dried her eyes and sighed. "I know you're right, Digby," she said finally. "Where do we go?"

Where they went was across the street. Next to St. Paul's parsonage, in a group of red brick, bowfront row houses in better condition than on Digby's side of the street, Digby had often noticed a small sign in a window which read MORRIS KESSELMAN, M.D.

In answer to their ring, a buzzer sounded which allowed Digby to push open the door and they entered a dark hallway with ancient but clean wallpaper. By following the wear on the Turkey carpeting, they turned right into a waiting room which seemed also to function as Dr. Kesselman's parlor. There was a large crank-up Victrola for entertainment and a considerable amount of over-stuffed furniture which, though old, was well cared for. Only the limp magazines betrayed age. There was no facility for a nurse. All in all, the room spoke for a modest practice, one which had commenced years ago.

Digby and Blossom huddled together in the center of a leather sofa and waited. From the floor above they heard the commotion of someone moving, then the quick heavy steps of someone descending a back stairway. A door in the back of the house slammed, and in a moment Dr. Kesselman was standing in his office doorway squinting at them with an expression of total ill temper. He was a heavy man in his late sixties, with sparse gray hair not yet combed. For a moment he stood polishing his thick glasses with a vigor that threatened to wear away the glass. A cigarette hanging from his mouth released a large ash which fell onto his pajama top, dissipating itself as it went until only the last few motes settled on his slippers. He wore dark trousers but otherwise appeared as though they had taken him from bed. He threw on his glasses and peered from Digby to Blossom and back, his expression softening a bit with his improved vision.

"Give me five minutes," he growled and disappeared back into his office.

Digby avoided looking at Blossom but he nevertheless heard a long sigh escape her. He played with several magazines in front of him but found he could not even look at the pictures. The doctor's five minutes stretched to twenty but finally he reappeared, clean-shaven, ready for the day, his cigarette now dropping ashes over a starched white shirt and black tie.

"Now," he asked gruffly, "who's the patient?"

Digby rose slowly from the sofa and cleared his throat. "We'd like to have some blood tests made," he said.

Dr. Kesselman raised his eyebrows and, without disguising his thoughts, looked straight at Blossom. With his thumb and forefinger he removed the cigarette to allow himself a spasm of coughing and replaced it.

Digby cleared his throat again and said. "We'd like to get married."

The doctor grunted, or laughed. Digby didn't know which. But he waved his arm indicating they were to follow him into his office. "Take off your coats and roll up your sleeves," he commanded. While they did this, he stomped around the room banging cabinet doors and drawers of instruments until he had collected what he needed. With his hands belligerently on his hips, he stopped to look at Blossom's belly again, causing his scowl to deepen.

"In this instance, ladies last. Sit!" he said, pointing out a low white stool to Digby.

Digby sat obediently and gave his arm to the doctor.

"Where do you live?" Dr. Kesselman asked, jabbing a needle in Digby's arm.

"Across the street," Digby replied. "Opposite the church."

"What do you mean?" said the doctor. "It's an abandoned building. You live in an abandoned building?"

"It's not exactly abandoned now," Digby said. "We fixed it up. Before I moved in, I looked up the owner and he said if I painted his store, I could live in the house until it's torn down."

"A humanitarian," said Kesselman. "May God smile on his enterprises. And your betrothed, this young lady, I assume she shares this fancy address with you?"

Digby nodded and the doctor finished. Abrupt in his manners, his hands worked gently and quickly. He waved Digby away.

"When are you due, dear?" Dr. Kesselman said to Blossom when she had replaced Digby on the stool.

"I don't know. When the baby's ready, I guess," Blossom said shyly.

"I've delivered hundreds, black, white, yellow, red," the doctor replied, "and not one came by appointment. Of *course* they come when they're ready. I mean, when does your doctor *say* it will come?"

Blossom shifted on the stool, looked away from the needle, and said, "I don't have any doctor."

When the needle failed to puncture her arm, she glanced nervously at the doctor and found herself staring into his fierce black eyes.

"But you go to a clinic?" he suggested.

She shook her head.

"From the beginning you've seen no doctor?"

She nodded.

"Oy!" he groaned and inserted the needle in her vein. He said nothing further until he was finished. Then he turned half towards Digby. "You know, if you have no money, there are places a person can go. Even after graft and red tape take their cut, there's a little left over for a free clinic here and there. This child is having a baby. Your first?" he asked Blossom. She nodded. "Her first!" he informed Digby.

"He didn't know," Blossom said quickly. "I didn't tell him."

"My dear child," Dr. Kesselman said impatiently, "in the beginning a man doesn't know. Later, he knows." He looked up and saw Blossom close to tears and Digby staring agonized at the floor between his feet. He rose and put the samples of their blood carefully aside. "Maybe your fiancé will not mind waiting for a few minutes for you in the other room since you have spared him the ordeal up to now. I want you to get up on this table, please."

Digby paced the waiting room from one yellowed etching to the next, not really looking at them, only filling up the minutes. For the first time he felt fearful for Blossom's sake. Finally, when it seemed to Digby that surely the morning was stretching into afternoon, the door opened and Blossom appeared, her color high, but her expression relaxed and happy.

"Digby, everything's all right," she said.

"If you're a believer in long engagements," Dr. Kesselman observed drily, "forget it. I want you to go from here to the city hall for a license. And don't shlep her on the streetcar. Take a taxi. You have money for a taxi?"

"I have some but I want to pay you," Digby said. "Please."

"Sometime come back and I'll let you paint one wall of my office," Kesselman replied. "Pay me by not being such a nitwit!" He walked them to the door. "If you go into labor today, don't call *me*. It's my day off. I usually have lunch with my broker and we go over my portfolio of riches I've made from this crummy neighborhood. Then I might go to the opera. Sometimes I fly to Paris to shop! But in absolute, positive emergency, sometimes I'm home. But don't call me. If there's a bad delivery some cousin of yours will convince you I should be sued for malpractice because I'm insured for millions."

Digby, as he stepped into the cold morning air, felt the man's heavy hand on his shoulder. "Don't worry," the voice behind him said. "She's a very healthy specimen. She had the sense to eat the right things. She doesn't fear her body. In my opinion, you are a nitwit, a jackass. I shudder for your unborn child. But you have good taste. As women go, you could have done a lot worse."

A trickle of ash cascaded down over Digby's shoulder and the door behind them shut with a bang.

By the time Digby flagged down a cab — they were scarce in the neighborhood — Blossom was frozen, but on the ride downtown to city hall, she thawed out in style.

"It's been ages since I rode in a car," she said.

"Sometime I'll rent a car," Digby said. "We'll go away for a trip."

"Digby, you *drive?*" Blossom said, surprised.

"Sure, I drive," Digby said.

"Funny, I can't think of you behind the wheel of a car," Blossom said, examining him with a fresh eye.

"Well, I can drive," Digby said, puzzled over the unreasonable irritation that came over him. Could he, he wondered? It had been a long time.

They had no trouble getting their marriage license. In fact, they found themselves getting preferential treatment.

The morning's events left Blossom in a thoughtful mood. When they returned home, she made Digby lunch but had none herself. Instead, she drank cup after cup of coffee and wandered silently but not at all unhappily between their two rooms as though she had never really looked at them before.

Digby threw his energies back into the happening. He began to worry, now that the happening was irrevocable, that only three days, including Saturday, were left to them. He filled a large thermos bottle with coffee and told Blossom he was going to the church to work on the lights. Running down the steps he unexpectedly came upon Dudley Harrison, who insisted he was just about to knock on the door and if it appeared that he was looking in the keyhole, it was because he had just bent over to tie his shoe.

"I know plenty about electricity," Dudley grinned. "I'll be glad to give you a hand."

Together they spread Bernard's lighting equipment out on the sanctuary floor. It was a discouraging collection.

"Nothing's going to come out of *this* mess," Big Mohammed said.

"Dudley, we're going to build a world of color out of this mess," Digby said with confidence. "But first we're going to have a cup of coffee. And while we drink our coffee, we'll think a little bit. And when we've had our coffee and thought, we'll begin. There's a kitchen in the parish hall. I'll get us some cups."

Left alone, Big Mohammed knelt furtively among the loops and tendrils of the wires that grew like vines in the patch of light. His eyes narrowed, and as they scanned the choir loft and the indistinct corners of the church they drew a milling audience of all Big Mohammed's enemies from hiding, from behind the empty pews, the organ pipes and stone pillars. In the crackle and

62

groan of the room's old timbers, Big Mohammed heard testimony to their mute and restless anguish. "This court," he said softly to these shadow-defendants, "is now in session."

He lifted a cable and showed its insulation bruised away, exposing a rainbow of fine wires like nerve endings.

"You all see this? Exhibit A," he informed the court. He held up the wire cutters. "And you see this? Exhibit B. If I put Exhibit A in the jaws of Exhibit B and give my hand just a *little* squeeze . . . Snip! Then that's all she wrote! Take them a month just to *count* all those loose ends!"

The rumble of Big Mohammed's laughter chilled the room. "The verdict is guilty, so we don't have to waste time on that," he continued. "Cutting up these wires, that's the sentence. Now comes the trial. I'm the prosecution. There ain't any defense. In Big Mohammed's court we do things a little different."

With exaggerated care, Big Mohammed set aside the cable and the cutters. "Now, I'm going to give you some evidence," he said thoughtfully. "Oh, I got evidence, from the cradle on. I got *tons* of evidence, but I don't have much time. Lots of things I won't mention, like my job with the moving company when the other men was always carrying out lamps and end tables and I had to carry out sofas and pianos, and when I said I'll take my share of pianos but I want my share of lamps and they said what you're going to get is your share of the sidewalk, so git! That's a long story. I got stories to fill a library. An uptown library, I mean, not a downtown library because they don't have so many books and half of what they *have* got is about Booker T. Washington! Man, I don't *ever* want to see another book about that man! I'll just pick out one of my stories from the hat."

Big Mohammed playfully laid a hand across his eyes and plucked something invisible from the air. He shook out this old sorrow like a bandana. "You're going to be crazy for this one," he smiled, examining it. "It's a good one."

Big Mohammed made a preparatory, "Ahem!" and threw a glance around his audience to draw them nearer. "It was like this, ladies and gentlemen," he began. "Day before yesterday I was down on Columbus Avenue and I see this old white lady, a hundred years old, trying to cross the street. I watch her a minute and I say to myself, 'Dudley, that old lady's going to get herself killed.' The way them cars was coming they wasn't even going to stop long enough so's her body could be dragged off to the undertaker. She'd lay there flattened out like an old cat until the sun dried her hide and the rain washed her away. So I goes over to her and I says to her, 'Lady, they're going to run you down sure. Let me take your arm and we'll cross over together.' You know what she done?" Big Mohammed asked, his voice suddenly low. "She whips out her umbrella and give me a *fap!* right over my head. She starts yelling her fool head off and then there's a police whistle, and there's old Dudley running down an alley with a lump on his head he wouldn't have had if he'd minded his own business! I never stole a purse in my life! Not a white lady's, not a black lady's. Never took a quarter from my own mama's purse! What's that old white lady giving me the business end of her umbrella for? Now you think about it. In your hearts, you got to admit that's how it's always been. Dudley Harrison tries and tries, and every time you just put it to him again. But now he's here in this light and you're in them shadows and the way I judges it, you *owe* him a few snips with these wire cutters!"

A heavy pounding was growing in Big Mohammed's chest forcing him to pause for several deep breaths. "You know I don't want to do it," he said, speaking with difficulty. "But I can't see the percentage in trying anymore. No *sir!* Everytime you gave it to me, I always said, 'Dudley, try just one more time. That's not asking for the world. Just one more time.' Then sure as I'm sitting here in this cold damp place where I've no business to be, in the middle of this junk that ain't going to amount to anything, you go right on and do it to me again! But that red umbrella was the livin' end! I've tried my last try!"

Big Mohammed fitted the knot of wires in the jaws of the cutters. Sweat glistened like varnish on his bowed face. In his ears the creaking of the room rose deafeningly as his enemies tumbled

65

over each other in silent outrage. "Snip, snip! That's all she wrote," he promised them. His massive hands gripped the cutters, but his arms began to shake uncontrollably. His sight blurred with tears. He knew that all the force of his will would not squeeze the cutters shut. "Lord, there ain't an ounce of justice in this world," he cried out. He threw the wire cutters clattering after the jubilant hoards of his escaping enemies. "All right!" he said hoarsely. "Now you listen! We are all going to try one more time! So damn you, you do right! This is your absolute, final last chance! Mr. Dudley Harrison ain't going to try but this *one last time!*"

As the silence of the room gradually ceased to have meaning, Big Mohammed felt a pleasant calm setting over him. Looking apprehensively in the direction in which Digby had disappeared, he wiped his eyes on his sleeve. "They got to say this for you, Dudley," he said with dignity. "You may be *bad*, but you ain't *mean*."

When Digby returned with the cups from the kitchen, he found Big Mohammed skillfully wrapping friction tape around the damaged insulation of the cable.

As the afternoon darkened into winter twilight, Big Mohammed found himself soldering and splicing wire under Digby's direction, nearly electrocuting himself in an effort to make things work. Bundled in his overcoat, Reverend Sitwell sat in the cellar with a supply of fuses and changed them as necessary, while on the floor above Digby and Big Mohammed leapt away from fountains of sparks and hissing serpentine coils of wire. Mrs. Jenks announced in the middle of the afternoon she was going home with a headache. She told Sitwell his supper was in the oven and he could heat it up at his leisure, unless they were also planning to play with the gas lines.

Finally, at seven that evening, Blossom was able to look across the street to find a strange new light shining through the round window of St. Paul's. More importantly, it shone steadily.

Inside the church, on the floor, Digby, Sitwell and Big Mohammed lay on their backs gazing rapturously upward, an empty bottle of sherry at their feet. In their ears was the steady, comfortable hum and clink of machinery, and up above them on the ceiling, moving masses of green and red swirled behind a rotating dome of stars. They lay watching for a long time until Big Mohammed's sonorous voice broke the stillness.

"I wonder, does anybody here think I could maybe . . . on Saturday night . . ." he began. "Course, it's just an idea . . . I mean, I just throw it out and you can throw it back at me. I won't be mad or anything like that if I can't. It just kind of come to me and I throw it out, but if you both think it's a good idea, why I'd be pleased to do it . . ."

"Do what, Dudley?" Sitwell asked curiously.

"Be a black Santa Claus," Big Mohammed said softly.

"It's a capital idea!" cried Sitwell. "What say you, Digby?"

When no sound came from Digby, Sitwell and Big Mohammed raised themselves and found he had drifted off into a peaceful, exhausted sleep.

Chapter 8

*T*hursday it thawed, an early winter day that seemed golden and warm as September. The powdery, loose snow began to congeal and squeak underfoot. Trickles of clear, sparkling water oozed into the street from snowbanks, forming puddles that reflected the sky like scraps of blue carpeting strewn carelessly down the length of the street. Blossom, her belly pressed against the glass, looked out and felt a need to be in the fresh air once more before the child and the winter closed her world around her. It was no surprise to Digby when she waddled down the aisle of the church with Cleo in tow.

"We brought you and Dudley your lunch," she announced.

She eased into a pew, breathless but cheerful.

"Where you off to?" Digby asked, not sure she should be out at all.

"Down to the Goodwill. Cleo and I thought we'd make ornaments for the tree if we can find some odds and ends."

Digby might have objected had the Goodwill store not been one of Blossom's most favorite places.

"Did you ask Reverend Sitwell, yet?" Blossom asked.

"I tried twice," Digby replied lamely. "This afternoon, I swear! If I have to gag him and sit on him!"

"Don't get excited," Blossom soothed. "I'm just asking."

Since the legal obstacles to his marriage had been taken care of, it had been on Digby's mind to ask Sitwell to perform the ceremony. A number of times he tried to lead Sitwell conversationally into the subject, but Sitwell was now as hard to catch and hold as a runaway balloon. He chased his new enthusiasm with such élan that Digby had been unable to approach the subject without being interrupted by a phone call, a visitor, or having to yield the floor to some new idea gestating in the old man's head.

Digby tried once that noon and twice in the afternoon but to no avail.

At supper, Digby watched Blossom picking at her food and asked anxiously, "You feel OK, baby? Anything happening I should know about?"

Blossom gave his hand a reassuring pat and replied calmly, "Not yet, Digby. I want to get the sheets washed and ironed first."

"I'll get Sitwell tomorrow," Digby promised. "Will tomorrow be all right?"

Blossom laughed. "You ask me every day," she said, "and every day is fine with me. Digby, you're the one who got me thinking about it. And the more I think about it, the better I like it. But you're the one that has to ask Sitwell. I'm leaving the paperwork all up to you."

"Tomorrow," Digby said firmly, making Blossom laugh at the resolute thrust of his jaw.

With supper out of the way, they made preparations for the evening's work. As with all Digby's projects, the first problem to be dealt with was Big Mohammed's pessimism.

"Nothing's going to come out of this mess," Big Mohammed said, eyeing the piles of torn newspaper strips Martha and Cleo were making and the bucket of paste Happy was stirring. "I don't see any bird coming out of this mess, no sir!"

Digby had no comment; he was blowing up an enormous balloon.

"Give it here," Big Mohammed said. "Let me work on it a while. That's if I got any breath left after hustling those pews all day. If that preacher doesn't stop finding more people to sing and dance and fiddle, the children will have to stand outside and look in through the windows!"

It was Cleo who had first suggested a piñata, and though the idea was impractical for so many children, Digby accepted it, feeling it important her suggestion be used. He passed the idea of a piñata through his head, enlarged on it, embroidered upon it, endowed it with philosophical overtones, and in the end had come up with a giant papier-mâché dove of peace.

When the balloon had grown to three feet, Big Mohammed refused to add another breath, and it was set in the center of a bed of newspapers.

"It's simple," Cleo said. "You dip the strip of paper in the paste and lay it on the balloon. Keep criss-crossing the strips for more strength."

In this fashion, with all hands working, the balloon became covered with the wet paper. Layer after layer, its hide thickened with old murders, riots, and stock market quotes. A smaller balloon for a head was covered and attached to the larger balloon with more strips.

When they finished, it was late in the evening and their hands were pink and crusted with paste, but even Big Mohammed was satisfied that here was a bird.

"But it looks more like a fat duck than a dove," he remarked.

"It needs trimmings," Martha said.

"A paper beak with an olive branch," Cleo offered.

Paper wings stretched out and crepe-paper feathers glued on, Blossom thought.

"That'll be one beautiful bird." Big Mohammed said. "It's a damn shame we can't make it fly."

Digby walked around the dove considering it, his smile deepening into a wide grin. "Dudley, you can make book on it," he said. "By the time we're finished, this bird's going to lay eggs!'

Chapter 9

*T*he next morning, Digby awoke conscious of a small but insistent buzz in his ears and a ticklish vibration that permeated his whole being. It was familiar and he knew what it meant. For days he had been running from one task to another, had been unable to close the door on one completed thought before another had slipped in, and like the Queen in *Alice*, had believed six impossible things before breakfast. Digby had long ago set his inner alarm system in order and now, like a teakettle beginning to whistle, it warned him that a few minutes off the fire would be beneficial.

"I thought I'd take a walk up to Christmas city this morning," he told Blossom, meaning uptown.

Blossom had already recognized Digby's mood from the maddening wiggle of his toes under the blanket. "I'm glad. Enjoy yourself," she smiled.

"Anything you want?"

"Let's see," she thought. "Will you be going as far as the Haymarket?"

"I can."

"Then, something for Christmas dinner," she decided, and taking down their coffee can, she gave him a few dollar bills.

"What shall I get?" he asked. They both knew he was not a clever shopper, and what he held was not the price of a Christmas goose.

"Buy whatever appeals to you as long as it feeds five," she replied. "If a sixth turns up, I'll be taking care of it myself. If you buy meat, just make sure it's not green. If it's fish, hold it under your nose." She suddenly had an additional thought and shook up the change in the bottom of the can, picking out three quarters for Digby. "We need a package of white crepe paper for feathers. Go to the easiest place. There'll be mobs of people, Digby. Are you sure you want to go?"

Digby shrugged. "Sure, I'll go. Anyway, I promised Rudolph I'd be back before Christmas."

"Oh, Digby," Blossom laughed. "Do you know why I'm standing here not able to button my bathrobe."

"Why?" he grinned.

"Because you're a man who keeps promises to deer!"

When Digby reached the sidewalk, he found the sky an endless, unmarked blue. Raising his arms over his head, he took several deep breaths of cold air and touched his toes a few times. Feeling bet-

74

ter immediately, he set off in the direction of Christmas city.

Digby enjoyed his own company. It was not that he enjoyed loneliness. Loneliness was sad, destructive; he had not been lonely for a long time. But solitude was something else, and he had learned the wisdom of weaving healing patches of it into his life. When he overworked or his life became harried, he had learned to expect a blunting of his senses. Cataracts of dullness grew over his eyes. Too often he found himself asking Blossom to repeat what she had just finished saying. His focus blurred, causing so much that might have pleased and excited him to pass unnoticed and be lost forever. It was in these times that the buzzer in Digby's head sounded and it was then that Digby excused himself, took a few deep breaths, and invited himself out for lunch.

The air seemed still fresh from the recent snow and Digby walked quickly. There was too much to be done at the church for him to make a day of it. When he reached the park, he crossed through it without stopping then to see Rudolph. He paused only once, to look at the edge of Christmas city seen through the trees. The faces of the shops were bright with electric stars. In their windows, mannequins were frozen in the act of decorating gold and silver trees. To Digby, who had thought of it during the long walk as a place of infinite delights, it now suddenly seemed a place to be avoided; yet the crepe paper was a necessity, so he left the park and crossed into the shopping district.

He chose the closest department store. A mistake, he soon realized. When he had found the crepe paper, there was no choice but to stand in a long line of people holding ribbon, gift wrapping and candles. The line inched along slowly toward the cash register, but Digby felt, after looking at the faces around him, that such a general malaise had fallen over Christmas city he would not risk beginning a conversation with a stranger. He filled the time instead by watching a nearby display of television sets, fascinated by the unfolding history of a fat woman curiously dressed as Pinocchio, down to a set of cardboard ears and a long nose on which was perched an artificial bird. Although she was winning things, she was always encouraged to trade these winnings for the unknown contents of an envelope, a box or a curtained compartment. The master of ceremonies was Mephistophelean and cool, but to Digby it seemed that this strange Pinocchio and the mob of other bizarrely dressed onlookers did quite a lot of jumping about. By the time Digby's turn came at the cash register, the lady was agonizing between two curtains. The music blared, the drums rolled, and the chosen curtain opened to reveal not an automobile but two tickets to Las Vegas and a set of matched luggage. Digby sighed, watching Pinocchio's black eyes shrink into pinpoints of disappointment. She made one or two half-hearted hops but her glee had evaporated. There were times he found the world incomprehensible, Digby reflected.

Noon was not far off and Digby took a shortcut through the financial district into Dock Square, discovering an acre of trees for sale. Real trees. It lifted his spirits to have left the plastic ones behind. On the other side of this wood he emerged into the Haymarket where pushcarts, makeshift stands and noisy hawkers choked the street. Digby, who loved the excitement of the Haymarket, found it already teeming with holiday buyers, though the workingmen would not be free to shop until evening. The walkways were narrow and slippery underfoot with crushed vegetables and the fat from meat markets, all of whom set trays of frankfurts, pigs' feet or glistening tripe outside their doors. Digby allowed himself to be swept along, hearing music in the babel of tongues around him. Everyone shouted; no one was angry.

At the other end of the short street, the human stream buoyed Digby into the sunlight where he saw wagons of mums, poinsettia and a weathered cart missing most of its blue paint. The cart was imaginatively patched with parts of vegetable crates but was serviceable, since it now sagged with a load of fresh clams covered with a blanket of crushed ice. Lunchtime, Digby decided.

"How much?" he asked of a rosy old man tending the cart.

"All you want. Fifty cents," the fellow replied agreeably. "If you ain't too hungry."

Pocketing Digby's coins, the clam man produced a paper plate and a small knife. Digby watched the knife effortlessly split open the shells which the man set on the plate, careful not to spill the juice.

"Take lemon and hot sauce," the man directed, handing the plate to Digby.

There were only one large communal lemon and one bottle of hot sauce to be passed back and forth between the diners, but at last Digby could tilt back his head and let a clam slide off its shell into his mouth. The clam juice dripped down his chin from his moustache, cold and wonderfully fragrant. The clam slid down his throat like liquid ice, the lemon puckered his mouth, the hot sauce left a glorious trail of fire that reached to the soles of his boots.

Oh, my God, he thought, here was food to shake up the soul, to raise the dead even!

With eyes watering from the hot sauce, he asked for a second plateful, and finishing that, he bought three dollars worth of clams Blossom could steam for the household's Christmas dinner. He needed now only a head of lettuce.

In a short time, Digby had reentered the park and stood patiently to one side until there was an opportunity to see Rudolph alone.

"Hey, Rudolph," he called. "It's me, Digby, again."

Rudolph's ears wiggled at the rustle of the paper bag from which Digby took a head of lettuce. In a moment, he came cautiously to the fence.

"Your nose looks pretty good," Digby said, glad to see the red paint had nearly disappeared. "You see? I'm surviving. You're surviving. You won't

78

even have anything to explain to your old lady when you get home." He tore the lettuce apart, gave some to Rudolph, and threw the rest to the back of the pen. "You've got beautiful eyes, Rudolph," Digby smiled. "With eyes like that you ought to be populating the whole North Pole. I won't see you again until next December." He reached out and passed Rudolph's soft ears through his hands. "You have a good year."

Digby picked up his clams and crepe paper and turned to view the lights of Christmas city a last time. Then he walked quickly away toward home.

Oh, so much to do, he thought happily as he walked.

The buzz was gone.

Chapter 10

*A*dding cardboard wings didn't make the duck into a dove, nor did the gluing on of hundreds of crepe-paper feathers. In fact, every addition — the beak, the olive branch, the large blue eyes — only furthered the illusion that here was a gross but splendid error of creation, some lapse in the mysterious logic of evolution. A roc or a phoenix? Maybe. But a dove? No. It troubled no one.

Digby and Big Mohammed inserted a piece of two-by-four through a slit they made in its back. Into the two-by-four they screwed a large hook that was in turn attached to a long rope leading upward to the highest crossbrace near the peak of the roof. With its insides crammed full of penny candy, they were finding the dove only slightly less trouble to launch than a laundry basket full of cannonballs.

Perched in the choir loft, Digby and Big Mohammed straddled the wooden railing, each holding a side of the dove. With beads of sweat standing out on his forehead, Digby chanted, "One for the money, two for the show, three to make ready, and four . . . to . . . GO!"

They released their hold and the dove swooped down over the pews below like a giant pendulum. It reached the low point of its flight and then continued on, gracefully rising up and up until it crashed into the front wall behind Sitwell's pulpit with a depressing loss of feathers. As it swung back to Digby and Big Mohammed, they leaned far out over the edge and managed to grab enough of its hind parts to drag it back to safety.

"It's too damn heavy!" Big Mohammed said. "If it doesn't take down that front wall, it's going to bust itself to pieces."

Digby bit his lip and thought. "It shouldn't swing back and forth anyway," he decided. "It should fly in a big circle so that when we pull the tab on the bottom, the candy gets sprinkled all over the audience, not just down the middle. Let's try heaving it off to one side. In fact, you'd better do it alone," he suggested, "because tonight I'll be down there working the lights. Here, stand on the railing."

Big Mohammed looked down at the floor suspiciously.

"I'm not much for high places," he mumbled, but nevertheless he achieved a teetering stand on the railing. "Hold onto my coat, man! I got to have somebody up here tonight to hold onto my

Santa Claus coat. I got to be steady," he said firmly. "If I fall from here, I'll go right on through to the cellar."

"There's going to be a choir on both sides of you and a string quartet behind you," Digby promised. "Somebody will hold you."

Big Mohammed turned half around to scan the choir loft. He wobbled dangerously on the railing, clutching Digby's head. "Digby, there's no *room*," he pleaded. "They'll be in each other's laps!"

"There has to be room. Sitwell says they're coming. Now give that bird a hard push off to the right."

Big Mohammed held the rope with one hand and with the other gave the dove a solid push at its rear. They froze in their places while the dove flew in a long ellipse around the edge of the sanctuary. The return half of its flight was done backwards but that couldn't be helped. When it reached them at the end of its first circle, they allowed it to sail past and begin a second revolution.

"That's beautiful!" Digby cried. "Perfect! I'll pick it out with a blue spot."

"It's going to sail around about five good times," said Big Mohammed, pleased with his efforts. "Is that time enough for all the candy to fall out?"

"Plenty," replied Digby. "Just be sure to pull the tab before you launch it."

"A dove dropping down the blessings of peace," laughed Big Mohammed. "I swear, Dig, you're a genius."

Digby shrugged and flipped through the scribbled papers on his clipboard. Below them, a group of black singers began to drift in for a rehearsal. "Let's find Sitwell," Digby said.

They located the old man in his study, listening on the telephone. They settled in deep leather chairs and waited. From the church came the sound of voices singing.

"On this day, everywhere, sounds of joy, fill the air . . ."

"That's the message," Digby said softly. "Sounds of joy."

The minister's face, when he hung up the phone, had a bewildered expression. "What do you make of *this?*" he asked. "That was the mayor's office. His Honor's looking in on us tonight."

"Election year," Digby explained drily.

"So it is," Sitwell recalled. "I suppose one of his ward people suggested he come. Well, I say good! Let the mayor see this corner of the city is coming to life. We have a few votes here, and a good many needs."

"There's nothing going to come of *his* visit," Big Mohammed said. "He's not coming to look. He's coming to be looked *at*."

"Our happening is for everybody," Sitwell reminded them. "Even the mayor. He won't be staying long. He's lighting trees for people all over the city. I told his secretary we had no tree but we were releasing a dove of peace later in the evening. She thought that would be a nice change."

83

Digby looked at his scribbled notes with a frown.

"Maybe we could go over our bag of tricks," he suggested. "I've lost count of what there is."

They had already agreed on a rough division of labor. At the door, Big Mohammed would function as the official greeter in his Santa Claus costume. At the climax of the evening, he was to launch the dove of peace as the four massed choirs blew off the roof with Randall Thompson's "Alleluia."

Digby was to play the lights like an instrument, flooding the church with colors and projections as the unfolding happening required.

This left Sitwell to function as a kind of floor manager. He would decide when the moment was ripe for the audience to rise and sing a carol, and when it was time for the Unitarian girls' dance choir to leap into the aisles in black tights and animal masks for the manger ballet. Was the time right for the reading of *A Child's Christmas in Wales*, or was it better given to the appearance of the three Christmas spirits to Scrooge? When was "Silent Night" to be sung and when should the Magi be sent through the audience? Which things should happen concurrently, and which in sequence? The groups had rehearsed separately and had not yet seen one another. Most of them would have to wait behind the doors leading to the parish hall until they were cued by Sitwell's blinking flashlight. Spontaneity was the essence, Digby had taught, and Sitwell accepted this. "But I'll need your help," he said. He was suddenly unnerved by all the elements his telephoning and visiting had turned up, and reaching into a desk drawer, he produced the inevitable bottle of sherry.

The three men had shared many glasses of sherry over the past few days. Sometimes it served to relax them and sometimes it was to keep their sinking spirits afloat. Either way, it seemed to work.

Though there were still several hours to go, Big Mohammed decided he would get into his Santa Claus suit. Digby excused himself to look in on Blossom. When he reached his side of the street, Digby turned and looked back at the church with satisfaction. He had discovered an awning in the basement, and though it had been a nuisance to put up, the flapping red tunnel gave St. Paul's an air of elegance, provided one were not standing downwind. The odor of the mildewed canvas was strong enough to support the canvas *without* its framework of pipes.

Digby found Blossom had put on her best flowered shift and was combing out her freshly washed hair. "Everything all set, honey?" she asked when she noticed him in the doorway.

"All set," he smiled. "The dove's hung up and ready to fly, the lights are all set, Dudley's climbing into his red suit, and Sitwell's primed with a glass of sherry."

"I've made some fresh coffee, if you want some," Blossom offered, slipping on long silver earrings Digby had once given her. Digby nodded and began to sit down on the mattress.

"Digby, don't sit there," Blossom said quickly. "I just put on clean sheets."

"Oh . . ." Digby said absently and leaned against the wall watching Blossom pour his coffee and listening to her softly humming to herself as she did it. "Clean sheets?" he cried out suddenly.

Blossom laughed, offering him his coffee. "Yes, Digby," she said calmly. "Today is the day."

"Oh God!" he said hoarsely. His hand shook so violently that Blossom took the coffee cup away from him.

"If you want me to make an honest man of you," she gently suggested, "it had better be soon. I'm in labor."

"Oh God!" he said again and ran to the door. "Get yourself ready," he shouted. "I'll be back for you!"

"Digby! I *am* ready," she called down the stairs after him. "Digby, I'm coming right over!"

Digby rushed past Mrs. Jenks and burst into Sitwell's bedroom just as the old man was finding how well his silver hair looked with the black turtleneck sweater he had bought for the occasion. The agonized expression on Digby's face gave him a fright. "Digby, what's happened?" he cried.

Digby had run, leaped, and at times, flown from Blossom's side to Sitwell's. His chest heaved, his head throbbed, and the room persisted in going black in front of him except for Sitwell's eyes which looked piercingly into his own. "Married!" Digby gasped. "Blossom and me!"

"Oh, Digby!" Sitwell beamed. "I'm *so* pleased. My heartiest congratulations!"

Digby shook his head and swallowed. "No, I want *you* to do it," he said, clutching Sitwell's shoulders.

"I'm honored," the old man said emotionally. "Tell me the date and I'll put it on my calendar this minute."

"Right now!"

"Today?"

"Now!"

"Oh, Digby," Sitwell said doubtfully. "It's already such a full day. Do you think you should?"

Digby shut his eyes and nodded. "Man, I'm positive!"

From below came the sound of the doorbell and, in a moment, garbled voices among which Digby heard Blossom's.

"I haven't done a wedding in years," Sitwell said dubiously. "I wonder if I remember."

"Fake it," Digby pleaded.

"Well, come along, then," the old man said heartily. "We'll all muddle our way through. It *can* be done. You've taught me that, Digby."

"We appreciate it," Digby said gratefully.

Sitwell, assuming command of the situation, led Digby directly to the study. "Mrs. Jenks!" he called out before him, "A fire, if you please. We are going to have a wedding."

Sitwell smiled hospitably on Cleo, Martha and Happy, then went straight to Blossom. "My dear young lady, how very pleased I am to be of service," he said, warmly kissing her cheek. "What a pretty bride!"

Mrs. Jenks, leaning over the woodbox, released an armload of kindling that fell clattering to the floor.

"Please make yourselves comfortable," the minister begged. Noticing guests and principals alike were standing in awkward silence, he shook hands with everyone at least once and announced, "An informal wedding is the finest kind to my thinking. Mrs. Jenks, how long has it been since you and I had a wedding in this room?"

Mrs. Jenks twisted her apron, hovering so close to tears that Sitwell hastily answered his own question. "Many years, of that I'm sure."

"Ho-ho-ho!" a deep voice cried from the hallway, and following it, a red apparition appeared in the study doorway. "*I* know who's been good and who hasn't!" the apparition grinned at the wedding guests.

St. Nicholas was pleased by the flurry his visit occasioned and offered his knee to anyone who wanted to tell him what he wanted. "Course, I ain't making any promises," he informed them, "not until I run your Social Security number through my IBM Goodness Computer."

Sitwell located a copy of the wedding service and blew the dust from it. He glanced over it and put it aside. "I'll do it not by heart, but *from* the heart," he said. He asked to see the license. Digby's face went white, but he saw gratefully that Blossom was drawing it from her bag.

"I'm sure it's in order," Sitwell said, setting it on his desk. "Now, you have the rings?" he asked Digby.

Digby paled again and this time Blossom was not able to help. "I don't have any," he said hopelessly.

Sitwell's face became momentarily thoughtful. "Well, then that's a bit of luck," he said. "*I* have some. They were my mother's and father's. They were to be my wedding rings but since that event is now beyond its season, it would be a kindness to me if you would have them. Mrs. Jenks," he said, "they are in my stud box tied together with a piece of ribbon. If you would be so kind?"

With Mrs. Jenks dispatched for the rings, Sitwell positioned Blossom and Digby in the center of the room.

"The maid of honor?" Sitwell asked, and Cleo stepped forward. "The best man?" Sitwell inquired, looking at Digby.

Digby's face went blank once more, then brightened as he looked at Big Mohammed. "Dudley, would you do it?" he asked. "I'd be pleased to have you."

Behind his white cotton beard Big Mohammed's face was inscrutable. "Me?" he asked, in disbelief. "You want *me?*"

"Please," said Digby.

"I could run and get you somebody," Big Mohammed said quickly, "if you just say who."

"I don't want anybody else," Digby insisted. "You're my friend, man."

Big Mohammed's beard quivered but he answered loudly, almost belligerently, as though there were some possibility of contradiction, "I *am*. I surely *am*."

Sitwell arranged the four in a row with Digby and Blossom a little to the front. When Mrs. Jenks returned with the rings to see the arrangement, anchored on its right by Santa Claus, large tears welled up in her eyes. Sitwell decided against asking her to render the wedding march. The piano was sure to be out of tune and Mrs. Jenks's wrong notes had a way of increasing as fast as the powers of ten once the first one was made. And Wagner became Shostakovich.

Sitwell untied the ribbon linking the rings and gave one each to Cleo and Big Mohammed. To Digby and Blossom he said, "Now, please join your hands."

A hush fell over the room broken only by the crackling of the fire Happy had quietly finished making and the purring of Emmanuel, who sat on the mantel among the candlesticks and porcelains, overseeing all like a genial household spirit.

Sitwell clasped his hands in front of him, smiled warmly at his small congregation, and began.

"Dearly beloved," he said, his voice strong, assured, very much the shepherd, "we are gathered together in the sight of God . . ."

Chapter 11

*B*lossom had lost track of how long they had been sitting this way — Digby against the wall and she against him. Twilight became darkness but Blossom would have endured agonies not to disturb the circle of Digby's arms around her or the pressure of his face against her hair. How many gifts this man had to give her, she thought. More than the seed of their child. More than the warmth and tenderness of his presence. In the silent dark, she acknowledged he had given her the most elusive of gifts — the gift of herself, a person she could love because he loved her. With her fingertip she traced his hand resting flat against her belly, feeling the strong delicate bones under the skin, the softness of the relaxed muscles and the ribbons of vein. What an unfathomable miracle was a hand, she thought.

"Digby, our life will change now, won't it?" she asked softly, breaking their long silence.

"Life should change, baby," Digby replied. "We change with it."

"I'm not afraid," she replied, and felt an answering pressure in his arms. She allowed herself a moment longer, then reluctantly unwound herself from Digby's arm, rose, and turned on the light.

"It's time, Digby," she said. "You'd better go. You have your happening to take care of and I have mine."

"I don't want to leave you now," Digby said miserably.

"Cleo and Martha are waiting for the doctor," Blossom argued. "Now, Digby, go over to the church. Please."

She smiled with such assurance that Digby couldn't think of any reason why he should stay except that he wanted to be nearby.

"But you *are* nearby," said Blossom. "We'll send Martha to you if we need you."

At that moment, Cleo and Martha burst into the room flushed and out of breath. "The doctor's coming right away," Martha said, and Digby saw Blossom's face soften with relief.

"You see?" Blossom said. "Everything's set now. Please, Digby. Martha will run over every half-hour to let you know our progress."

Martha nodded and reached for Digby's parka, which she put into his arms. Digby kissed Blossom and patted her belly. "For luck," he said, "and because I love you."

At the window, Blossom watched him reappear below. He was now walking fast and by the time he crossed the street, he was running, leaping the snowbank on the opposite gutter with the easy grace of a high hurdler. He disappeared under the red awning and Blossom smiled, praying her new husband wouldn't change no matter what course their lives now took.

When he arrived a few minutes later, Dr. Kesselman stomped around the room, muttering to himself, glaring at the one dangling light bulb and the mattress where Blossom lay.

"I have a lot of water boiling," Cleo said to him timidly.

The doctor stopped his pacing abruptly and focused his glare slowly on Cleo. "Good!" he said finally. "Make me a cup of tea."

"Do you need anything else?" Martha asked. "If there's something you need, I can run out for it."

Dr. Kesselman looked around the room and heaved a long, discouraged sigh. He pulled a ring of keys from his pocket and gave them to Martha. "This one is my house key," he said. "Bring me a chair."

Chapter 12

*D*igby went directly to the front of the sanctuary where a tangle of wires, rheostats, and machinery comprised his horseshoe nest of operations. In this one-man orchestra pit where he would play his lights, he settled himself on a low stool. He took off his watch, laid it on his knee, and mentally rehearsed the light cues on his clipboard once more. The box of projections and the colored gels were put in order. Every uncommitted moment sent his thought homing to the room across the street, to Blossom. He consulted his watch again. Ten minutes to eight.

Digby looked over the congregation behind him. The sanctuary was half full even though the large groups from neighborhood houses, social agencies and the House of the Holy Sojourners were yet to come. But the choir loft was crowded. Both choirs were in place, and at the foot of the round window the members of a string quartet sent out threads of sound as they tuned their instruments. In front of the quartet, Digby made out Happy, his guitar slung over his back, trying to drape two black choir robes to hide the dove which was tethered back at the railing ready to fly.

Digby knew he was better off occupied, and partly for this reason and partly because he hadn't eaten, he set his watch and clipboard on the stool and went towards the parish hall in search of a cup of coffee.

If the sanctuary had an expectant hush and dimness about it, the hall at its rear was a hive of cheerfully bossy women. They shouted directions to one another and rushed across Digby's path with plates heaped with cookies. On tables already groaning with plenty, fat, aproned ladies set buckets of crushed ice in which were buried bottles of pop. From the kitchen, the smell of spiced, mulled cider simmering on the stove hit Digby's nose with the force of a blow.

Lean young dancers limbered themselves, solemn-faced and oblivious to their choreographer who wandered among them with a harried air, crying, "Hold onto your masks, please! I want everyone to keep their *own* mask *right in their own hand!*"

Across the room Digby saw Pearl building pyramids of red and green doughnuts.

"Well, I see you got Dudley Harrison out there working," Pearl laughed when Digby came up. "I've been nagging him to get a job for a long time and wouldn't you know, when he finally does it, it would be seasonal work."

"It's a beginning," Digby shrugged with a laugh. "Any extras?" he asked, looking hungrily at the doughnuts.

"As many extra as you want," Pearl replied.

Digby took one red and one green doughnut, requisitioned a cup of coffee, and picked his way among the singers and dancers, passing through the door separating the parish hall from the sanctuary. As he elbowed the door shut behind him, he was startled to see a beam of light shoot up from one of his spots. It lasted a second and then went out. It wasn't Dudley. He could hear Dudley's booming "Ho-ho-ho" coming from the vestibule and Sitwell wouldn't be touching the lights. Digby hurried to his nest and saw a small, thin boy of about eleven examining the switches on his light board.

"Hey, I know you," Digby said in a friendly way.

The boy stiffened guiltily and said, "I didn't touch anything."

"Cool it," Digby said, sliding onto his stool. "No harm done."

Without realizing it, by sitting down he had effectively sealed the boy's exit from the horseshoe arrangement of lights. "You live at the Sojourners," Digby said. "Remember? The night you wanted me to take the kitten?"

"I remember," the boy said.

Digby watched the child's eyes glance furtively

to the left and right of him. *Alabaster*, he thought again. No other description fitted this cold, white, but luminous and rare face.

"I came back and took your kitten," Digby said. "I guess you know that."

"You looking for a medal?" the boy asked coolly. "It wasn't our cat. It wasn't anybody's."

Digby shrugged. "Want a doughnut?" he asked.

The boy considered the doughnut a moment, but said finally, "I have to go."

Digby withdrew the doughnut and glanced behind him. The house was now full to overflowing. Not far away were about twenty children from the House of the Holy Sojourners, divided at intervals into manageable groups by the placing of Sisters.

"You can sit here with me," Digby offered. "Pretty crowded over there."

"I'm not sitting either place," the boy replied matter-of-factly. "When the lights go out, I'm cutting out."

"Oh? Where're you going?" Digby asked conversationally.

"Out."

"The Sisters will miss you," Digby argued mildly.

"I always get back by bed check."

"But they lock the gates, don't they?"

A hard smile formed on the boy's face. "I can get in. I get in and out of that place like it was my own house."

"They're good doughtnuts," Digby said. "Why don't you have one?"

97

"I have to go."

"Well, you might as well wait until the lights go out," Digby said. "It's almost time."

Digby reached for his watch but the gesture failed halfway and he looked curiously at the clipboard on his lap. He remembered picking it up from the stool to sit down and he realized now that there had been no watch on it. He groped around the floor at the feet of the stool, found nothing, and looked up into the unblinking eyes and mocking half-smile of the child.

Digby looked into the haunted eyes and a part of his will hardened. *Oh, no, my little friend*, he thought. *Yesterday, and maybe tomorrow. But not tonight!*

"What's your name?" Digby asked evenly.

"What do you want to know for?"

"That's a crazy name."

"That's a dumb joke."

"What's your name?" Digby asked again.

The boy sullenly considered Digby, sensing a subtle change in him. Finally he yielded to the tension of the moment and mumbled, "Dennis."

"Well, Dennis, you look hungry," Digby said. "You take this doughnut and you sit down there on the floor and you eat it."

If a rebellion were coming, Digby knew this was the moment for it. He saw anger and fear in his prisoner's face, but though his own expression remained cool, impassive, he was pleased by what he saw. Even alabaster might be heated, flushed with color. *Well, Dennis, if I'd kicked your ass, you could have handled it*, Digby thought. *But I didn't, and now what are you going to do?* Digby sipped his coffee with unconcern, and over the rim of the paper cup he examined Dennis and wished that they were somewhere with a good light, paints, and a blank canvas.

Then, with a heroic display of indifference, Dennis took the proffered doughnut.

Digby tossed his parka to the floor. "Bundle it up," he said. "Make a pillow to sit on." Dennis wadded the parka carelessly, knelt on it and bit into the red doughnut.

Digby felt a hand on his shoulder and looked up to see Sitwell. "Is it time?" the old man asked. "We're full to the rafters!"

"I've lost my watch somewhere," Digby said casually. "But we're ready anytime you are."

"Then I'll give the signal," Sitwell said nervously. "Good luck to us all!"

Digby watched the old man circle around to the back of the church and with his flashlight give a signal to someone Digby could not see. Instantly, the slow, measured thunder of a kettledrum began.

A stillness like the settling of dry leaves came over the audience. The organ picked up the beat of the drum with triumphant music. Digby looked down at Dennis.

"Come here, Dennis," he whispered. Dennis looked up suspiciously. "Come here, man! I want you to do something." Dennis got up and Digby put the boy's forefinger to a switch on the light board. "You didn't get your doughnut for nothing," Digby smiled. "When I tell you, and not before, you press this switch."

Imperceptibly, the room darkened. Digby scanned the rows of small, fading faces. *Come on, little ones, open up!* he pleaded inwardly. *There are more wonders in the world than you can guess at this minute!*

As the room became totally dark, the organ marched up the scale with splendor and color. Digby's hand dropped gently to Dennis's shoulder. On the top note, Digby said, "Now, man!" Dennis's finger pressed, and the graying, patched, cracked ceilings and walls of St. Paul's became the infinite blue space of a Bethlehem night. Dennis gasped at what he had done, and the audience made a subdued "Aaaaaaaahhhhh" of surprise. Digby's spirits were immeasurably lifted.

Doors on either side of the altar platform were flung open and from the parish hall marched robed singers. *"Come, all ye faithful, joyful and triumphant,"* they sang vigorously, each singer holding a candle that swayed hypnotically as they filed around the outside of the sanctuary, circling the audience with flickering light.

"I'm going," Dennis said.

"Not yet!" Digby growled. "Sit down!"

When the final verse of the carol began, Sitwell reappeared. "Next we'll have the Swiss bell ringers," he whispered to Digby. "Then I'll lead the audience in 'God Rest Ye, Merry Gentlemen.' That will set a mood and give time to get Scrooge and the Christmas spirits in place."

"Roger!" Digby said, and fell to work setting the lights for the Dickens with meticulous care. This was Sitwell's masterwork. He had adapted it himself and rehearsed his little company to distraction, distilling the essence of *A Christmas Carol* to five characters and ten minutes' playing time. And if the result was a style of theater not seen on the boards since Lotta Crabtree toured the frontier saloons, Digby felt Dickens somehow survived.

Out of the darkness, Digby heard Martha ask, "How's it going, Digby?"

"So far, so good," Digby replied, almost frightened to see her.

"Same with us," Martha replied in a businesslike tone.

"What does that mean?" Digby asked anxiously. "What's happening over there?"

But Martha had gone.

Digby and Dennis watched Scrooge forge a halo out of his chains, and the evening continued on, smoothly, but not perfectly. Once a fuse was blown, but the audience was hardly aware that the pitchblack was not scheduled since the choirs were then singing "Watchman, Tell Us of the Night." Sitwell had been farsighted enough to station Mrs. Jenks at the fuse box and in due time night gave way to dawn without incident.

If Digby had an inclination to worry, he lacked the leisure it required. Dividing his attention between Blossom and his work only caused him burned fingers from the hot lights and punctured gels which he set Dennis working frantically to repair. Sitwell abhorred a vacuum and always set one event in motion before the one before it was finished. Digby needed all his wits and both hands to keep up with him, and sometimes a borrowed finger or two from Dennis.

"Didn't expect to work, did you?" Digby said to him once in a low voice.

"I don't mind," Dennis had replied in a tone, which, if not friendly, was not openly hostile.

When Happy rose in the loft to sing his finished carol, Digby, for a few minutes, was able to relax in the simple lighting needed. In Happy's carol, a stranger wandered in search of the Holy Child. The refrain asked simply of each new encounter, *"Are you the Child? Are you the Holy Child?"* While Happy sang, Digby played a baby spot over the audience, pausing sometimes on a baby held in its mother's arms, sometimes on a wide-eyed grinning boy, sometimes on a teenager.

"You want to work the spot for a while?" Digby whispered to Dennis.

"I can't," Dennis protested.

"Sure you can," Digby insisted, and reaching down, pulled Dennis to his feet and put first one of his hands and then the other to the spotlight. The brilliant circle of light jumped crazily over the walls of the room before it settled under Dennis's trembling hands. "Be careful, it's hot," Digby cautioned as Dennis began to guide the spot down the rows of children as Digby had done. "That's it. A little slower. Just a little slower. Hold a face until something happens to it," Digby said. "Watch how a face opens up sometimes when the light shines on it."

Digby drew his sleeve across his forehead and sat back on the stool watching Dennis's total concentration in his work. When Dennis glanced fleetingly over his shoulder at Digby, Digby nodded approvingly and whispered, "Good boy!"

The boy turned back without comment except a slight hardening of his face against the praise.

"Are you the Child? Are you the Holy Child?"

Digby gazed at Dennis whose mouth had dropped open slightly. Pinpoints of light, leakage from the back of the spotlight, played over his cheeks, eyes and hair. He seemed now so absorbed, so open and unguarded.

We always meet in the dark, alabaster child, Digby thought. *Shine the light on yourself. Let me see. Are you the Child? Are you the Holy Child?*

When Happy's final notes dissolved in the air, Sitwell's flashlight blipped a signal in Digby's eyes. Digby sent a wide blue spot to the head of the center aisle where a startled shepherdess hastily crammed a papier-mâché sheep's head onto the last of her sheep and began dancing her flock down the center aisle to Bethlehem. The Bethlehem road proved very dark, for Digby and Dennis were scrambling around on their hands and knees trying to retrieve the light cues which had slid off Digby's lap to the floor.

Besides being dark, the Bethlehem road was

short and very soon led the sheep into an innyard already overcrowded with pirouetting cows, oxen and geese.

Two oxen collided in a sickening crunch of papier-mâché, setting Digby and Dennis off on a fit of sniggering. Through his tears, Digby tried to scan the crumpled pages on his lap but it was hopeless. "To hell with it," he whispered and threw them away. "Wow!" he exclaimed. "Here come the Magi. Dennis, take this box of gels. Do what you can for the manger. I'll spot the Magi."

Digby swung a bright pink beam to the Magi, who, in their borrowed blankets, turbans, and love beads, made an altogether impressive display. Ancient Melchior, his snowy beard reaching his belly button, was distributing gold — five dollars in new pennies — back and forth among the pews. Fat young Gaspar passed out lighted sparklers and black Balthazar sprayed lily-of-the-valley myrrh from aerosol cans on both sides of the aisle. Above the taped soul music to which the animals danced, Digby could just make out the voice of Melchior passing out his treasure. "Here, kid. Here's a penny," he said jovially. "Here you go, curlytop. Have a penny. Don't spend it all in one place. Hey, anybody doesn't get a penny, raise your hand!"

Digby looked around to check Dennis. The boy had given the manger a flesh pink glow and now knelt absorbed in the action, forgetting his lights. The dance had become quiet, a mere swaying of kneeling or reclining animals around Mary who writhed on her bed of hay, her agonies silent but cruel, evocative of the force of life that drew the infant Jesus from her womb. The animals lowed softly, the music sank to a bare rhythmic whisper, the audience, still as in sleep, sat unblinking. Forgotten by Digby, the Magi stopped on the road to watch. Digby's arms dropped to Dennis's shoulders and he yielded his senses entirely to the color, the movement, the sound, and felt the art of what he watched become for a space full-blown and natural life. The animals covered Mary with a canopy of their arms, and when they opened like an unfolding flower, the child was free. Mary raised herself. Joseph bent over her. And when the mother lifted the child to his father's arms, time stopped for Digby. The most ancient of trinities stood clear in his eyes, not as dogma but as the design of men's lives.

The animals rose. They began to dance and life dropped quickly back to art as the family, the Holy Family now, led a procession off the dais to the parish hall.

Unfortunately, the Magi arrived at the innyard a little late, out of gold, out of sparkling frankincense, and dry of myrrh. They stood awkwardly, empty-handed and superfluous, looking after the last cow, like three gaudy Arabs who had just missed the Orient Express.

"No news, yet," came Martha's hoarse whisper out of the darkness, but when Digby turned there was no more of her to see than a slim dark shadow weaving its way to the door.

Sitwell had considered a dozen of his parishioners to read *A Child's Christmas in Wales*, had secretly engaged them in conversation to listen to their intonations, and then had chosen himself. As he listened to the rich, plum-pudding prose of Dylan Thomas, spoken with the alternating hush and power of the little man's voice, the rolling *r*s and the terminal *t*s crisp as finger snaps, Digby knew the choice had been right. If a criticism had to be made, it was that a phrase now and again was garbled by an excess of sentiment in the reader.

At the conclusion, Dennis, who had sat very still throughout, stirred and turned toward Digby. "You believe all that jazz?" he asked solemnly. "You believe anybody ever had a Christmas like that?"

Digby reconsidered the gruff uncles startled out of their naps by popping balloons, the aunts fragile as faded teacups, the tea laced with rum, the crystal cold, the caroling, the mistletoe that hung from the gas jets of the Thomas's ruddy Christmas house, and said, "Yeah, I believe it. Don't you?"

Dennis shrugged and for a moment inventoried his beliefs. "I might believe it right now. Right while I hear it," he finally agreed, grudgingly. "But I won't believe it tomorrow. And Christmas *Day* I won't believe it."

Digby made a gesture of acceptance. "That's what an artist is for, man," he replied. "While you read his book, look at his picture, sing his song, you *believe*. And it's good to believe. It's *essential* to believe." Digby smiled into the boy's face and pushed the hair out of his eyes. "You don't know what I'm talking about, do you?"

"I guess not."

"That's OK," Digby said. "I don't always make sense. I tell you what. You come to see me sometime. I live in the beat-up house across the street. Just drop in. Have a cup of coffee with us and we'll talk. You can play with our cats . . . hey, I'll let you hold my brand-new baby. How about that!"

Dennis nodded. "OK," he agreed softly.

I truly want you to come, Dennis, Digby thought, tracing with his eyes the inspired line of the black silhouetted face in the darkness. *I lose nothing. I sacrifice nothing. At this minute, it's the idea of you I love. But if you come I may learn to love the Dennis of you, too. When you look at my five-dollar watch, you skinny, deserted, ill-used, beautiful little punk, remember me, and that I have cats in my broken-down house!*

They worked for a while in silence, confining themselves to essential questions and directions, each absorbed in his own thoughts. But then Digby heard Dennis call his name softly.

"Digby?" the boy called apprehensively. "Look at what I found on the floor! A watch! It must be yours." He crawled towards Digby on his knees, the dangling watch held out in front of him.

"Oh, Dennis," Digby groaned.

Ignoring the watch, he impulsively pulled the

107

boy roughly into his arms and imprisoned him there in a tight bear hug. He felt the thin body stiffen with fear, and in the midst of his joy, part of Digby stayed profoundly sad, knowing how little the child had felt affectionate hands. "Thank you, man!" he said over and over. "Thank you, thank you."

"It's a good watch," Dennis mumbled, extricating himself from Digby's arms. "Must be worth something."

"At least a million," Digby said humbly.

"Good thing I found it," Dennis said airily. "Somebody could've clipped it on you."

Chapter 13

*T*he time had come for the dove to spread its blessings. Digby and Dennis were ready to throw millions of pinpoint stars overhead, and in the choir loft, Digby could just make out a big red Santa pulling away the choir robes that had hidden the dove.

Coming faintly at first, and then stronger, over the sound of choral voices, was the wailing of police sirens.

"Nothing yet," Martha's voice said to Digby from the gloom.

"Why does a baby take so long to come?" Digby whispered.

"Blossom's really beginning to come on strong, now," Martha reassured him.

"Don't worry, Digby," Dennis said cheerfully. "My mother had lots of kids. There's nothing to it."

The approaching sirens became very loud, then fell to a whimper and died in front of the church.

"The mayor," Digby said to Dennis without enthusiasm.

Sitwell had heard it, too. Digby saw his small black figure move along the far wall of the church to the church door.

Sitwell was unprepared for the entourage that traveled with the mayor. Hardly had he introduced himself when half a dozen photographers pushed past him, along with the mayor's wife and two large policemen. For a second, Sitwell was blinded by flashbulbs set off in his face. When his vision began to return, he found the mayor, a large red-faced man, scowling into the church. "It's so *dark*," His Honor was complaining.

"Would you call yourself a hippie priest?" a reporter asked Sitwell.

"Not *now*," said the mayor petulantly. "I'm behind schedule." To Sitwell he said, "On behalf of the people of this city, I want to thank you for asking me and my family to join in the festivities. Now, you've got a dove of peace or something you want me to release, is that right?"

Success had strengthened Sitwell. It popped into his mind to say, "You invited yourself, you booby!" But enough perspective remained for him to say instead, "It was kind of you to find time. Yes, we have a dove. Follow me, please. Our dove is in the choir loft."

Sitwell set out with the mayor at his heels and, looking back over his shoulder as he mounted the narrow stairs, he found the whole ménage was following. "It's a very small loft," Sitwell tried to suggest. "Perhaps some of you might watch from below." But the crush of photographers behind him pushed him on ahead. Reaching the top of the stairs, they climbed over the singers to the center of the loft where they found Big Mohammed looking nervously over the edge of the choir loft.

Seeing the dove, the mayor asked unpleasantly, "What's that? I thought it was a live one in a cage." Then he saw Big Mohammed. "Oh, for Christ's sake," he mumbled under his breath. His wife pulled her fur coat close around her and turned in slow circles, making sure her official grace fell on all parts of the loft. She was also trying to make clear in her own mind which was the way out.

The dove and Big Mohammed delighted the photographers. They scrambled over the loft like monkeys, getting in the singers' way, tumbling over each other, competing for the best angles. Sitwell wondered what their pictures could possibly show except each other's elbows.

"What do I do?" asked the mayor.

"The dove symbolizes . . ." Sitwell began.

"Gentlemen, get a shot of me with that window in the background," the mayor interrupted.

"The dove symbolizes . . ."

"Yes, it does," the mayor smiled. "Now what do I do?" he asked again, consulting his watch.

"You give this bird a push off to the right," Big Mohammed interjected sullenly. Now that the

111

time had come, he resented this theft of his big moment.

"Does *he* have to be in the pictures?" the mayor asked Sitwell.

"Not if you want to stand up here," Big Mohammed said, patting the railing.

"All right. Shall I push it now?" the mayor asked, stepping forward. "Ready, boys?"

"Not *yet!*" cried Big Mohammed. I got to get up here." He climbed shakily onto the railing. "Somebody hold onto my coat," he said anxiously.

"Your Honor," a photographer yelled. "Hold up your arms like you're just ready to push the dove."

The mayor lifted his arms and made a smile as jolly as Father Christmas.

"Somebody hold my coat!" Big Mohammed said, more loudly.

"OK, Mayor!" someone cried, and a blitz of flashbulbs lit the loft.

The mayor stepped dazedly ahead with his arms up and shoved the first thing he felt which happened to be not the dove but Big Mohammed.

Big Mohammed pitched into space, saved from sudden descent into the upturned faces below only by his death grip on the rope emerging from the dove's back. With the strength of desperation, he swung his legs up to seat himself on the bird's back; whereupon the dove and Big Mohammed, listing heavily to the right but not totally devoid of the poetry of flight, parted company with the choir loft.

"*Allelui-aaaahhhhHHHHHHH!*" screamed the four choirs, supplemented by Big Mohammed's howl of rage. Like a mounted Mother Goose he swooped down over the audience which ducked under the pews and shrieked with terror and delight. Digby covered his eyes. Sitwell dropped to his knees where he stood, too horror-struck to pray.

The front wall loomed suddenly up on Big Mohammed, who barely had time to put his feet out in front of him to save the dove. He hit the wall feet first with a resounding crash, left two large foot-shaped holes in the plaster, and by shoving with all his might, he was now speeding back whence he had come with more velocity than he had started with.

"All right, mother, if *that's* the way you want to play!" cried Big Mohammed, "LOOK OUT!"

The choir loft rushed towards him. He was vaguely conscious of the scrambling mass of humanity squirming over itself to get to the back of the loft. Held high above it, bobbing like a cork in a tempest, was a fragile cello. There was the sweet but fleeting image of the mayor's jaw hanging slack and then what seemed to Dudley Harrison the end of the world. There was the deafening crash of splintering glass, popping flashbulbs and the human outcry of those being swept through the window into the night. Digby, conscious of a profound silence, and feeling a blast of cold air, took down his hands; Sitwell opened his eyes. All they saw was a shower of white paper feathers and a length of rope swinging back through the opening where the window had been. On the end of the rope was a short length of two-by-four. In Digby's ears was the wild cheering, the whistling, stomping, tumultuous applause of the audience. "A happening!" Digby breathed.

Across the street, Blossom stirred on the mattress at the sound of the explosion. "What was that?" she asked groggily.

The doctor, at the window, replied, "You wouldn't believe it. I saw it and I don't believe it."

"Tell me," she said.

Dr. Kesselman reluctantly left the window. "Santa Claus, a big white duck, the mayor, a cop and two photographers just jumped through the window of the church into the awning. I'm a Jew but personally I like a more traditional Christmas." He looked down at Blossom and smiled. "A regular Flo Zeigfield, your husband." He got down on the floor and nodded encouragement. "You aren't doing so bad yourself," he said.

Chapter 14

In the middle of the uproar, Digby had fled the church. For an hour he had been sitting on the top step in front of the door where Blossom lay. There had been some activity shortly after he had gotten there but that was all he knew. The room behind him was maddeningly quiet.

On the stairs below Digby huddled his household. Martha leaned her head against the wall; her eyes were closed. Happy strummed idly on his guitar and sometimes hummed. On the step below him Cleo listened, a faint smile on her lips, her head leaning against his knee.

They sat this way, without speaking, until Sitwell and Big Mohammed arrived bearing a large covered tray.

"We've brought some coffee and some sandwiches Mrs. Jenks made," Sitwell offered. "We would like to keep vigil with you, Digby, if we may."

"Please," Digby replied. After a time he shook off his preoccupation to ask, "Everything all right at the church?"

"Oh, yes," Sitwell said. "A few minor cuts, nothing more. I daresay the mayor will turn it all to his advantage. And the children, Digby! You should have seen. They were ecstatic."

On Big Mohammed's face were several strips of adhesive plaster which he touched gingerly. "That mayor, he's something else," he growled. But the memory of his falling through the awning onto the grunting mayor, while a hail of gumballs and Tootsie Rolls beat around their heads, caused him to add more cheerfully, "Personally, I was very moved."

Behind them the door opened and Digby looked up from the step to see Dr. Kesselman.

"Well, Mr. Bell," the doctor said, "now you can come see what I've brought in my little black bag."

The doctor shut the door softly behind them.

Digby asked, "Blossom?"

"See for yourself," the doctor smiled. "Sleeping. A constitution like a peasant." He dragged his chair beside the mattress and nodded for Digby to sit down. "It's a new invention," he informed Digby drily.

Digby sank to the chair and watched the doctor separate a small bundle from Blossom's arms. He placed the bundle in the curve of Digby's arm and delicately separated the blankets a bit. "Your son," he said. "Son, your father. A nitwit, but all things considered, not a bad fellow. He will teach you. You will teach him." He walked to the door. "Only a few minutes now," he said, and left Digby alone.

Digby looked down at his son and eased the bundle securely into his arms.

The child looked up at Digby with a very old, wise expression. Its fragile, white, perfect hand slipped from the blanket and lay against Digby's work-roughened hand. Digby looked at the two hands, listened to the imperceptible breathing of the child and learned from these things the joy of his own manhood.

Blossom stirred luxuriously in her sleep and drowsily spoke a few unintelligible words and Digby's name.

Digby bent as close to her as he could. "I'm here. What is it, baby?" he whispered.

"Digby," Blossom said, almost inaudibly, "the house is so *warm*."